PERSONAL ESCORT

A BILLIONAIRE SECRETS STORY

AINSLEY BOOTH

WWW.AINSLEYBOOTH.COM

For all my readers who have ridden the TTC and just went, hey, is that Toronto's St. George Station? Yes, dear reader, it is!

SHE NEEDS A FAKE FIANCÉ.

HE'S SECRETLY FALLING IN LOVE.

Cara Russo needs to get married. Or at least, make it look like she got married.
Toby Hunt can't let his best friend's little sister rush into anything foolish. So when she needs to hire an escort, he says he'll take care of it.
Now he's waiting for her at St. George Station.

BILLIONAIRE SECRETS

Personal Escort is the second book in a sexy new rom com series!

READING LIST

Personal Delivery - Jake & Jana
Personal Escort - Toby & Cara
Personal Disaster - Marcus & Poppy
Personal Interest - Ben & Skye
Personal Proposal - Astrid & Brianne

www.ainsleybooth.com

This modern-day fairy tale first appeared in the *Love in Transit* anthology. This single title edition has additional chapters and a bonus epilogue.

The LiT anthology has now been retired, but paperback copies are available at book signings from the authors who participated: Jana Aston, Raine Miller, Liv Morris, BJ Harvey, Kitty French, and myself. If you pick up a copy at some point, I hope we get a chance to meet in person so I can sign the story that was originally titled *St. George Station*, and is now *Personal Escort*.

Happy reading!
∼ Ainsley

CHAPTER ONE

TOBY

Toronto
St. George Station

End of June

I SEE her before she sees me, and I'm glad to have a second to process how stunning she is before she realizes I'm the man she's here to meet.

The dress is perfect, the skirt flowing around her legs as she gets off the subway, the rest of the chiffon molded to her slim, delicate frame. Her hair is swept up off her face, but she's left it long in the back, and her golden waves catch the overhead light in the underground station.

People are looking at her, but she doesn't care, and that changes *how* they look at her—with awe, and whispers. *Do you know who that is? She must be someone...*

And she is.

Cara Russo. Grad student, secret badass, and a billionaire whisperer to boot.

My best friend's little sister, too.

And for the next hour, my pretend bride.

Or more accurately...I'm her pretend groom.

I adjust the boutonnière on my lapel. That's what she's looking for. I was in charge of the flowers.

You'll be wearing an orchid on your suit jacket, and you'll have a small bouquet for me, too. That's how I'll know you're my fiancé. I'll look for the flowers.

She's turning in a slow circle now, scanning the crowded platform. Her eyes are on the guy in the suit five bodies away from me. No, not him.

He doesn't know how special you are.

Keep searching.

She glances in the other direction, then stops. Her back straightens and her head tilts to the side.

Turn around.

I should be nervous about this. She's not going to understand.

Come on, Cara. Turn around and see me.

Anticipation zings through me as she turns slowly. Somehow, I'll find a way to explain what I've done.

I've got the flowers, after all.

I'm the escort she's hired for the afternoon. She just doesn't know it yet.

CHAPTER TWO

CARA

New York City
Upper West Side

Beginning of May

ONCE A MONTH, I fly home to New York City to have lunch with my Nana.

The rest of the time, I'm a data nerd studying at The University of Toronto. A coffee addict with no social life to speak of, and no complaints about that fact.

My monthly trips may seem excessive to most people, but most people haven't met my Nana.

She's a battle-axe. She turned her husband's failing business around, and then after he died at the age of thirty-five, married four more times. Each new relationship was a strategic business move. Mergers and acquisitions.

For forty years, she ruled as the CEO of Gladiator, Inc.

Now that dubious honor falls to my brother, Ben. But she's still on the board of directors, and as we discuss on a monthly basis, she wants me to take her seat.

I definitely do not want to do that.

But I love my Nana, so I tolerate that discussion, if only because it distracts her from her other serious concern about my life—that I haven't gotten started on my own merger and acquisition with an acceptable male specimen.

"I'm not even dating anyone, Nana," I remind her as I reach for the sandwiches.

She snatches the tray away from me. "Maybe because you keep stuffing your face."

I roll my eyes. "Pretty sure you can't get fat on watercress sandwiches."

She pins me with a hawkish glare. "Men don't like women who are lippy, either."

"Their loss." I'm going to have to run these rules past Toby. No sandwich padding, no lippy-ness... They don't sound right, but on the other hand, I'm not dating anyone.

And when you're twenty-four and not dating, there are some needs that start to make themselves apparent.

Not merger and acquisition level, though. More like...small scale experiments. A pilot study to determine feasibility of...I'm not sure what.

Having sex with a guy without making a fool of myself. Yeah. That would be a good place to start.

My grandmother keeps talking as if I hadn't taken a weird detour in my thoughts to Perv-town.

"What do I need to do to sweeten the deal, young lady?"

I laugh. "Nana, I don't want to sit on the board."

"Have you looked at the stock options?"

"I don't care about stock options." I hold up my hand. "And

don't tell me men care about that, too. I don't want to date a tycoon, or a banker, or...anyone like anyone in our family."

"You want us to leave you alone to that laboratory at the university in that country." She sniffs in the general direction of Canada, like the country stole me away from her.

The truth is, I jumped at the chance to put an international border between me and my family.

"Is that really so awful? Ben and Elena are happy to carry on the family business. I'm the baby. Nobody cares about what I do."

Nana gasps. "I care."

"You have a funny way of showing it," I mutter, lunging for the sandwiches.

She doesn't stop me this time and I take two, just to show her who's the boss of me. *Me*. That's who.

"I understand your grants for next year have not yet been approved," she says silkily.

Noooo. I drop the sandwich I was about to take a big bite out of. I give her a horrified look, terror streaking through me. "You wouldn't."

Seventy-five years old. A matriarch of a New York establishment family. And pure evil. She shrugs. "I would."

"Nana!"

"I want you married, and I want you on the board. It only meets quarterly. The rest of the time you can play scientist." She lifts her teacup into the air. "We'll discuss this again next month."

Okay, I'm not the boss of me. Nana is, and she knows it. That's...not ideal.

I glare at my tea, wishing I could turn it into a triple shot latte. "No, let's discuss it now. You can't...how did you even... please don't mess with my academic life!"

"Please get married." She gives me a bland, unwavering look.

"I could get other grants." I could use my trust fund. I could quit my program and run away with the circus.

I have options, but that's not really the point here. The point is that my Nana—crazy, bossy, bitchy, but still my grandmother, for better or worse—has decided I need to be married.

So I let her think she's won. I nod slowly. "Okay. Look. I'll be open to the idea. How's that?"

She narrows her eyes at me. "No funny stuff."

"Of course not. But you must understand, these things take time."

"Never took me any time."

"Well, I'm not nearly as cute as you were. Please don't mess with my funding, and I'll say yes to anyone who asks me out on a date. I'll drop broad hints about my love of peonies and white lace. Make sure to dress to accentuate my birthing hips."

"Don't be crude, Cara."

I'm pretty sure anyone who would be willing to marry me might like a bit of crude, but it doesn't matter. I'm not actually going to be asked out. I'm not actually going to do any of that.

Despite what Nana said, I'm totally, one hundred percent going to resort to funny stuff.

CHAPTER THREE

TOBY

GENERALLY SPEAKING, I'm a good guy to work for. I like my staff, treat them well, and respect their intellect.

Except for when they're being total idiots.

I swallow my curse, because I don't want to horrify the grandmother sitting across from me on the first-class flight from Los Angeles to New York. Then I take three stabs at composing the message I really want to write. ***Get your fucking acts together, or there will be hell to pay when I get back from this trip.***

But that wouldn't be productive, so instead I find diplomatic, but clear words to convey my frustration that once again we've hit a snag in the development of our new Bluetooth solid state memory device.

Our annual shareholders meeting is three weeks away.

Getting this right is not optional. If we don't have something new to announce, the forecast for the next two quarters will tank, and that will be fucking bullshit.

I don't like bullshit.

In the long run, I'll ride it out—and actually, I'd make bank on that slump, because I'd buy up stock released by people that don't have vision.

But it would be a distraction.

I don't like distractions, either.

I've never been one to play fast and loose with my business just to make money. I have more money than I'll ever need. Last year, I permanently endowed a national math camp for kids, eight to twelve.

No, I don't need money. I need stability and calm so I can focus on what really matters—making kick-ass products that change the tech industry. That's all that matters, and—

"Sir? We're in the final descent. You'll need to put away your laptop."

I can feel the flight attendant hovering beside me as I furiously finish typing. As soon as I hit send on a second email, this one to my chief engineer, I close my laptop and flip her a grateful smile. "All done."

She points to my utilitarian canvas messenger bag. "If you don't mind stowing it under the seat in front of you..."

"Of course not." I put it away and pull out my phone, which is already connected to the wireless network. The signal will cutout at ten thousand feet, which means I've still got a couple minutes.

I don't bother to look out the window. I've seen this approach into New York a hundred times at least. My best friends live here. I have constant business dealings here.

But ten years ago, I headed west and found my fortune in Silicon Valley.

Plus, I have the Pacific Ocean on my doorstep. It's hard to beat that.

I open the secure messenger app I use with Jake and Ben.

Toby: In town. Dinner?

Ben's name immediately pops up in a bubble.

Ben: You know what I appreciate? How much notice you always give us.
Toby: You aren't a woman I'm trying to impress.
Ben: I'm not even going to touch that.
Ben: Okay, I will. Jesus, I feel sorry for the women you date.
Ben: But yeah, I'm free for dinner. Wait… No, I'm maybe not. Hang on, Cara's messaging me, too. She's in town.
Toby: Invite her along.
Ben: Obviously I'm having dinner with my sister. The question is, does she want to extend the invite to your miserable, anti-social, ghosting ass?

The wi-fi cuts out before I can point out that Cara has more in common with me than she does with her brother.

When we land and my phone reconnects to the network, a dozen messages spill in. Jake excusing himself from dinner because he has plans. Ben making fun of my skills with women—which are perfectly acceptable, thank you very much.

Just because I choose not to use them that often, doesn't mean I don't know how to leave a woman with a sex-drunk smile on her face at the end of a very long night.

I just have other priorities most of the time. Saving the world, saving my parents, building an empire.

And tonight, dinner with two of my favorite people in the world, because Ben's also sent the name and address of the restaurant Cara has picked out.

Ben: She's fine with you tagging along.

It wasn't that long ago Cara was the one tagging along, not that I ever minded. Even as a teenager, Ben's youngest sister was sharply curious, a clever girl who had no time for ridiculous drama or hormone-driven conflict.

Toby: Of course she is. You'll be the one left out.

Six years ago, Cara moved from New York to California to attend Stanford University. For four years, she was literally down the road from me, and across the continent from her over-protective brother and sister, her controlling grandmother, and her self-absorbed parents.

So when she was picked up by campus police in her sophomore year, she called me to bail her out. That was the first secret that bonded us.

Then she applied to Masters programs around the country, and only got into Columbia. Instead of accepting it and moving back home for two years, she begged me for a job so she could buy another year of applying to programs further afield.

I gave her an internship. Secret number two.

For a bunch of reasons, I gave her a position on a different campus from where I work.

Reasons like how she grew the hell up over her four years at Stanford, her body blooming to finally match her very grown-up mind. If I wasn't careful, Cara could be a dangerous temptation to do something stupid.

Extra-stupid, because she persists in calling me her brother-from-another-mother.

Plus there were other reasons, like wanting to avoid a nepotism charge Cara didn't deserve. She was as qualified to be a Starfish Instrumentation intern as any other Stanford grad.

And there was never any risk of her trying to work her way up through the company. All Cara has ever wanted is to be free as a bird, and I will always do anything in my power to protect that for her.

Keep her out of New York City? Check. Be an understanding ear when she needs to vent? Check.

I'll be the not-quite-a-brother she's always wanted. The one who gets her. The one who supports her, no matter what.

CHAPTER FOUR

CARA

I MAY FLY home to New York to visit my Nana way too often, but I know better than to stay with her.

Instead I alternate between staying with my brother and my sister. Ben's place has the advantage of being quiet, so I stay there if I've brought work with me, or I need to study.

This weekend there's no such need, so I stay at my sister's townhouse just a few blocks away from my grandmother's. My entire family lives in a six-block area on the Upper West Side. Even my parents have stayed in here, which means my mother has spent the last twenty years bumping into a non-stop parade of my various stepmothers.

I swear my parents are the most fucked-up people in the world, and any credit for me and my siblings turning out to be normal human beings is full credit to Nana.

I put the finishing touches on my makeup—well, lip balm and mascara over a touch of Elana's crazy BB cream that's all the rage, because it's just Ben and Toby for dinner.

But when your sister is the CEO of a cosmetics company, leaving her house with a bare face is just a non-starter.

I slip my feet into sandals and open my bedroom door just in time to see one of my nephews go sailing down the bannister to the second floor. A shriek follows, then cackling little boy laughter.

Staying at my sister's is also excellent birth control, as much as I adore all four of my nephews.

Four boys under the age of ten.

Elana is crazy, and I'm pretty sure she's pregnant again. It stopped being a big exciting announcement two boys ago, but I didn't miss that she begged off dinner tonight, opting to stay in with her family instead.

With four boys and a husband who encourages roughhousing? The only way she's skipping sushi with Ben and Toby is if she can't eat the sushi.

I know I'm right.

If I were a better sister, I'd say something. Tell her how excited I am for her—and I am. Offer to help out—which I could, because my program is flexible enough I could spend more time in NYC.

But right now, all I can think about is Nana's crazy demand I find a husband.

How the heck am I going to do that?

Not a real husband, of course. That would be insane.

I need a marriage of convenience. Maybe somebody who needs a green card and likes tea.

The din from downstairs grows louder.

"Unca Ben!" The excited cry is followed by a heavy *oof*. That would be the littlest one leaping into my brother's arms.

Right. Crazy plans will just have to wait until after sushi.

It takes Ben a few minutes to extricate himself from a spontaneous wrestling match, so by the time we get to Brooklyn, Toby is waiting outside the restaurant for us. He's standing back from the sidewalk, leaning against the building, and he's typing on his phone.

Always working, just like Ben. But there's something different about Toby. Maybe it's the fact he went to California, that he made a name for himself in an already crowded industry. That he did it on his own terms, in his own way. He owns a majority share in the publicly-traded tech company he founded. A billionaire at thirty, and a philanthropist to rival Bill Gates at thirty-five.

Or maybe it's that he's always seen me as more than Ben's little sister. When I was a teenager, he encouraged me to apply to schools not on the east coast, and ran interference when my family objected. He invited Ben to bring me out to California and arranged for a personal tour of Stanford.

And then there's all the secret times he saved my butt once I was out there, too.

Yeah, I definitely have some hero worship when it comes to Toby, so when I see him concentrating so hard his brow furrows and his mouth pulls tight, I don't get annoyed like I do with Ben.

I find myself wanting to know what he's worried about, and wanting to distract him, too, because it's Sunday night and everyone deserves a break.

I assume he didn't notice us get out of Ben's town car, but as soon as I'm within earshot, he smirks—still looking at his phone—and says, "Only Cara Russo would make us cross the river for sushi."

"I didn't make you do anything," I say lightly, stopping in front of him and covering his screen with my hand. "Plus, you like it when I pick restaurants."

He takes his time dragging his gaze from my hand, up my arm, to my face, and when he finally looks at me, he's grinning. I grin right back. Even in heels, I'm eight inches shorter than him.

Ben gently removes my arm and frowns, looking at me first, then his best friend, as if realizing for the first time that we know each other in a way that doesn't directly go through him. "When have you two gone out for dinner before?"

I roll my eyes. "I swear you think I'm still in high school."

"Aren't you?" He pulls a teasing face, winking at me, but I'm not sure he's completely kidding.

"I spent five years down the road from the Starfish Instrumentation campus, remember? I made him take me to the most expensive restaurants in Palo Alto."

"A few times," Toby says blandly. He doesn't return his attention to his phone, he just tucks it away. He ushers me toward the restaurant, pulling open the door as he lightly touches his hand to my shoulder. "After you, troublemaker."

I give him a cheeky grin. I'm hardly that, but anything that riles Ben up is good fun in my books.

"You were a teenager for half of those years," Ben mutters.

I should ignore him. He's such a typical overprotective big brother, and he's all bark, no bite. And we're talking about *Toby*. But it's not the Russo way to be mature with one's siblings. I give Ben a too-innocent look. "And an adult for the other half." Toby makes a choking sound and I turn toward the hostess. "Russo. Party of three."

CHAPTER FIVE

TOBY

I HAVE no idea what's gotten into Cara tonight, but she's on fire. Ben looks torn between confused and worried and irritated, and since we've spent the last fifteen years ribbing each other pretty hard, I'm tempted to let him suffer.

On the other hand, I've never molested his baby sister, and the upstanding guy inside me wants that record straightened out.

Unfortunately, there's a small part of me that is now stuck on a weird mental loop around the word molest and the saucy look on Cara's face.

What the hell is happening?

Half of those years she was an adult.

Fucking hell, that is not the right takeaway from that exchange.

Half of those years you could have—

Nope.

I grab the menu as soon as we take our seats. Thank Christ for drivers. "Who wants sake?"

"Not Elana," Cara murmurs, her eyes still twinkling.

That works as a conversation changer.

"What?" Ben leans forward. "Is that why she passed on dinner?"

I'm not following. "Is what why?"

Cara laughs lightly. "I think so."

Ben groans and rubs his fingers against his forehead. "That would explain the crackers she was munching on in our last meeting."

Cara gasps. "You had a saltines clue and you didn't give me the heads up?"

"It's only clear in hindsight."

I look back and forth between them a few times before Cara takes pity on me. "I'm pretty sure my sister's pregnant again," she says.

"For the hundredth time," Ben adds.

"Congratulations?" I ask.

Cara nods. "Oh, definitely for them! Although the noise level in their house is already insane."

Ben laughs under his breath. "You'd think Elana having enough babies for all of us would be a good thing, but this is just going to ramp up Nana's pressure on me to get hitched."

Cara's eyes go wide, just for a second, but she doesn't say anything to that.

It's the first I've heard of it, too, but unlike razzing him about work or women, I know better than to comment on anything Nana Russo says. To Ben, his grandmother is a saint who can do no wrong. And even if she's pressuring him to settle down, he'd still be hard-pressed to criticize her.

She's his mentor. Hell, she practically raised him, even before his parents split up.

"This is her fourth?"

"Fifth." Ben scrubs his hand over his face. "And it's a good thing. I'm happy for them." He grabs the menu and raises his hand. "Yeah, let's get some sake."

Sure. That's the desperate cry of a happy man.

I'm way out of my depth here. I don't get why he cares about how many kids his sister has, and I feel like there's a nuance I'm missing. That I should know, should be able to fill in, because we've been friends for more than a decade.

I try to remember how he reacted the last time she had a kid. Two years ago? That may have been when we were deep in the off-shoring project for tech support.

Time before that? No clue.

I've met Elana's boys. They're all carbon copies of her husband, in varying sizes. Ben loves them. He's had them all over for sleepovers.

He's a way better uncle than I'd ever be, even if I had siblings.

The closest I'll ever get to being an uncle would be if Ben had kids himself.

Jesus. Is his biological clock ticking?

Is that a thing for guys?

Frankly, I don't want to go there. I turn to Cara at the same time she turns to me.

"So, how's school?"

"How's work going?" She stops, laughs, and we try it again. At the same time, again.

Luckily, the waitress arrives with a bottle of sake. "Ms. Russo, this is from the chef. He recommends it with the tuna."

Cara turns pink and spins in her chair, waving her hand in the air at the grinning Japanese man behind the counter at the back. "Oh, how sweet!"

Two billionaires at the table, and it's the pretty grad student who gets the star treatment. I get why she likes this place.

She rattles off an order, upping the numbers on some of the sashimi when Ben gives her a raised eyebrow.

As we wait for our food, I pour drinks all around. Then we get talking about work, and school, and before I know it, we've polished off two trays of impressive sushi and sashimi.

Just as the waitress is taking our orders for ice cream to cap off the meal, his phone chimes. He looks at the screen and swears under his breath.

"Is it work?" Cara holds up her hand. "We might need to cancel that ice cream," she says apologetically to the waitress.

Ben shakes his head. "No, you can take the car back to Elana's. I'll grab a cab."

I clear my throat. "I could drop Cara off."

She gives me a grateful smile. "Oh, good idea. I wouldn't want to miss the green tea ice cream here."

"You've got your priorities sorted out."

Her head bobs emphatically. "I spent all afternoon having watercress sandwiches batted out of my hand. I've earned this dessert."

"What? Hold that thought, I need that story." I stand up and shake Ben's hand. "Good to see you, man."

"Sorry to run."

"I get it."

"I know you do. Hey, walk me out?"

I nod, then point at Cara. "Don't eat any of my ice cream. I'll know."

She winks. "Will you?"

I shake my head and follow Ben outside. Flatbush Ave. is busy tonight, and his car still hasn't pulled up.

He shoves his hands in his pockets and winces as he stares up at the sky. "Do I need to warn you off my baby sister?"

I laugh. "No. I swear, nothing happened while she was out in California. She was a kid."

"She's not anymore." He swears under his breath.

"Cara's beautiful, smart, talented...and not interested in an old man like me. At all. Don't worry."

"Yeah. It's just that she deserves more than a guy like us, you know?"

I frown, vaguely uncomfortable with that characterization—not that he's wrong. Workaholics who rush out of restaurants on a Sunday night make terrible boyfriends. And it's really just a matter of chance that this is Ben making a swift exit and not me.

Not that I'm in the running to be Cara's boyfriend.

The unsettled feeling grows, getting less vague by the second. I change the subject. "What's really going on?"

"I don't know. Ever feel like you blinked and aged a decade?"

Not really, but that doesn't seem like the right thing to say. "Sure."

"You don't, you asshole. You're having nothing but fun times out on the west coast."

I grin. "It's good for the soul. Maybe you should relocate Gladiator, Inc."

He growls. "No, it's not that. I'm just..." He trails off as his car pulls to a stop in front of us. The driver gets out, but Ben waves him back. He opens the back door himself before looking back at me. "Next time, give us more of a heads up that you're coming. And stay a bit longer. I miss your ugly face."

"Life is short, Ben. If you aren't happy, nothing wrong with making a change."

———

"Dare I ask what Ben wanted?" Cara asks when I rejoin her at the table.

"He reamed me out for not spending more time here." Not a complete lie.

She doesn't buy it. She searches my face, her eyes sharp and knowing. Our friendship might be sporadic and framed by a weird I-remember-when-you-had-braces age gap, but we get each other. "That wasn't what I was expecting you to say."

"Oh?"

Sharp and knowing, but not jaded. She blushes, a faint sweep of pink across her cheeks that makes the blue of her eyes pop even brighter. "I thought he'd warn you off me."

"He did that, too." This is a weird conversation, one we've never had to have before. I try to soften the awkwardness. "But in a half-hearted kind of way. Like you got to him with your teasing and he just wanted to set the record straight, not actually threaten me."

She hesitates as our ice cream plates are set in front of us. Three delicate scoops, one green tea, one red bean, the last, vanilla on her plate, and mango on mine. She lifts her spoon and touches it to the green tea scoop before pausing and glancing back up at me. "I *was* just teasing before. You know that, right?"

"Of course." And that's not disappointment swelling in my chest. "I told him as much."

"Good." She takes her first taste and makes a soft, satisfied sound that is way too womanly for my liking.

Or just womanly enough.

"Yum," she whispers, her eyes closed and her lips...

Her lips.

The tip of her tongue darts out and licks the soft, pink swell of her lower lip, and all the blood in my body reverses course.

No need to worry about oxygenating organs where there's a dick ready to stand at attention.

Hello, Cara's mouth. Nice to meet you. Toby's dick, ready to molest you.

I jam my hand against the table and cough. Jesus Fucking—

"Is it no good?" She asks, blinking her eyes open at me in confusion.

Nope.

No good at all.

I clear my throat and reach for my spoon. "I was just thinking about your brother," I say gruffly. Yep, Ben. Mr. Overprotective. Mr. Family Matters. Mr. Probably Wants a Baby. Yes. That's a good damper on inappropriate feelings. "I think he's two steps away from sending for a mail order bride."

She sighs. "My grandmother has given me the *thou must get hitched* speech, too. And today she ramped up the pressure, just like Ben said."

I frown. "Why?" Ben makes sense. He's thirty-five, and effectively the head of his family. I can understand his grandmother wanting him married. Hell, I can understand *Ben* wanting himself married.

But Cara's just a kid.

No, we're all very clear on the fact she's an adult now. An adult who was a kid last time I looked, and is way too young to be pressured into any forever kind of plans.

She screws up her face, then blinks open one eye and looks right at me. "I think I might have a solution, though."

Something about the way she's looking at me, like *don't judge me,* maybe, or *can I trust you with this* makes my chest tighten up. "What's that?"

She hesitates, then drops her gaze back to her ice cream. Another scoop, another indecent moan.

"You don't want to tell me?" I take a taste of my own ice cream. It's amazing. Sweet and creamy, with the unexpected Japanese flavors making the whole thing that much more interesting.

"Probably shouldn't."

"I won't tell Ben."

She flashes me an indecisive look.

"I really won't."

I get a small smile for that. "I believe you. You didn't tell him about the time I was arrested."

"Detained, no arrest record." I made sure of that.

"Right." She sighs and takes another bite before putting down her spoon and squaring her shoulders. "I hate dating."

Excellent. Never date. No man is good enough for you. The flare of jealousy is bright and fierce and even more unexpected than the grassy notes of green tea in my ice cream. Unlike the dessert, though, there's nothing sweetly delicious about my blast of possessiveness. It's wrong and inappropriate. "So getting married isn't on your radar?" I manage to grind out. "That's fine. Just keep being you."

Keep being funny and gorgeous and celibate.

"But Nana has a point."

No, she doesn't. "How's that?"

"Well not for me, exactly. But she wants this, and…"

"You'd get married just to make your grandmother happy?"

Her eyes go wide at the sharp tone in my voice.

My spoon presses hard against my palm, and I glance down, realizing I'm white-knuckling the metal.

"I don't know." But the way her voice falls, I know I've done exactly what she'd hoped I wouldn't—I've judged her, and shut her down. Damn it.

"Hey." I set my spoon down and reach across the table, brushing my fingertips against the back of her hand. Her fingers are so much smaller than mine, slim and long, just like the rest of her. I ignore the awareness that pulses deep inside my body as I touch her skin. "Sorry."

She shrugs. "I know it's a ridiculous reaction. It's just that my grandmother is everything to us, you know?"

I do. On one hand, this is a sign that I should continue to mind my own business and leave the Russos to their complicated family dynamic.

On the other hand, life is short. "How about we finish this up and take a walk? You can tell me what Nana wants you to do, and I'll do my best to not think it's a terrifyingly bad idea."

She laughs, a peel of joy that grows and bounces in the air around us.

I don't hear that enough. I slide my phone out of my pocket. "Hey, when are you heading back? I'm flying to Toronto tomorrow evening."

"I'm on a mid-afternoon flight." She gives me a small, regretful smile, but her eyes are still crinkled with laughter.

No need for regret. I'm already rescheduling my last two meetings. "What airline are you on?"

She tells me her flight details even as she gives me a curious what-are-you-doing look, and I fire off an email to my assistant with instructions to get me on that flight and bump Cara up to first class with me if she isn't already there.

"How long are you going to be in Toronto?" she asks as we make our way out of the restaurant and onto the busy Brooklyn thoroughfare.

"Just a day, same as here. I've got a string of meetings set up. Here, Toronto, London, Dubai, Tokyo. I'll be home again next week."

"Back to your lab high above the ocean."

"Yep."

"You're so lucky," she murmurs, her eyes going soft as she glances up at me.

I dodge us around a group of people, my hand in the small of her back. She points to a park at the end of the street, then I look back down at her again.

It doesn't take long to reach the park. Two blocks. At least a dozen sideways glances. I suddenly feel too big, a bit clumsy, and certainly out of my league, because now all I can see is Cara's soft, pink mouth. Her bright eyes and gorgeous face. The one thing in the world more beautiful than the Pacific Ocean.

I'm not sure what I'm going to do next. It's definitely going to be foolish.

And totally worth it.

CHAPTER SIX

CARA

TOBY KEEPS LOOKING at me as we enter Prospect Park. We're finally away from the noise of the street. It's dusk, and we probably can't walk for too long before it gets dark, but I don't leap into a conversation right away.

I slow down instead, and he matches my pace. His legs are longer than mine, but as we walk, that doesn't seem to matter. Every few strides our arms brush, and after the third time, I laugh nervously.

"Just spit it out," he teases me quietly.

Easier said than done. "You said Ben's practically ready to hire a mail-order bride," I say, drawing out the words.

"Yeah."

I take a deep breath. "I get why you think he might do that. I was thinking of it, too. For myself."

He stops abruptly in the middle of the path. "Pardon me?"

I turn around to face him. "Nana has decided I need a husband. To the point where she's making crazy threats if I don't show up with a ring on my finger soon. Why not cut out the messy parts?"

I don't think I've ever seen Toby speechless before. He has a million ideas a minute, often texting or emailing one conversation while having another in person. He can multi-task like no other.

But right now, he's not doing anything. Not speaking, not thinking, not working... just staring at me like I'm an alien.

"Say something," I mutter, feeling all kinds of foolish now that my plan has been voiced out loud.

His face pulls tight into an unexpected scowl. "You can't... it's not that simple."

Even though I feel silly, being told I can't do something gets my back up. "Are you being overprotective? Because you know how much I dislike that from Ben."

"If you thought you'd get it any easier by running this past me instead of him, you were flat-out wrong." His voice is tight, clipped. "What makes you think, at twenty-four, that you need to rush headlong into marrying someone you don't even know?"

"*At twenty-four?* What does that even mean?"

"You're too young to settle!"

"Says the workaholic staring forty in the ass who hasn't had a real relationship in...ever?"

"Not ever," he mutters. "And I'm only thirty-five."

"Is that the official age of adulthood in the deluded universe of Toby Hunt?"

"Have you even tried dating?" He lifts his hands in the air, like he might strangle me—and wouldn't that be a weird twist to an already strange day. Billionaire murders best friend's little sister in Prospect Park.

"Sure."

He drops his hands to his hips and gives me a disbelieving look. "That sounds like not really."

"Toby—"

"Cara, seriously. Find a nice boy and start dating him." His face twists, like he's forcing himself to be lighthearted about this. "Let things progress if you like each other, and when he gets down on one knee, make sure he knows your brother has two muscle-bound best friends who will kick his ass if he doesn't treat you right."

"Muscle-bound?"

He flexes his shoulders, his chest straining against his dress shirt, and I know he's teasing, but there's a lot more bulk under that blue cotton than I'd noticed before. Then he gives me a terse, crooked smile, and an instruction that knocks the wind out of me. "You should wait until someone lights you up inside."

Gee, I wish. But after I catch my breath, I make a scoffing sound, because really? That hasn't happened in twenty-four years.

"I'm serious." And I can tell he is, the way he's staring at me like this is the most important lesson he could ever teach me.

My square-jawed, clear-eyed, superhero in full-on big brother mode.

No, not brotherly. A different brand of protective know-it-all. Like he thinks from his hyper-masculine, alpha point of view that anything less than a lusty conquering just won't do.

In theory, he's not wrong.

In reality, it's just not that simple.

"I'm so not a romantic, Toby. But that's a sweet thought."

He frowns. "I'm not a romantic, either."

"You sure sound like one." I reach out and push my hand against his chest. I mean to shove him gently, but he doesn't move, and my hand just collides against hard, broad muscles.

Really hard. Extra broad.

My heartbeat gets louder. If I were the fantasizing type, this would be how a lusty conquering would start. Maybe not in the middle of a Brooklyn park.

Probably not with Toby, although any reasons I previously could list for why not are now escaping me.

Has he always been this tall? Yes. But didn't he used to be skinny?

Definitely not skinny any more. *Do you do CrossFit?* Not a good question to ask out loud while I'm stroking his chest. But he probably does. I bet all the California CEOs do.

Maybe I should have spent more time paying attention while I was out there.

Except I had dated at Stanford.

Disasters, every single time.

Equal parts of me being too awkward and nobody being quite as hot as Toby is right now. If I'd been up-close-and-personal with a college-version of *this*, I'd probably have tried harder not to be hopeless.

With extreme effort, I pull my hand back.

No. Crushing. On. Toby.

I've heard that sex drives kick in as women get older. I wasn't fully aware of the possibility of *my* sex drive kicking into gear in a single day, and revving quite so hard for just one guy.

One off-limits guy, who still hasn't said anything.

I hover my hand a few inches from his body, my palm itching to touch him again. Over and over again.

Then I step back and laugh, because whoa, that was weird. "So anyway—"

Toby reaches out and catches my wrist, his fingers looping around my arm in a gentle, totally breakable bond. He steps closer, and I stop moving.

He pulls my hand back to his chest, and keeps moving, until the gap between us is gone and he's curved over me, his hand in my hair. His lips are right above my mouth and every cell in my body is screaming *yes!*

I didn't see this coming. From the hammering of his heart against my fingers, he didn't either.

This is weird.

Weird and good.

Weird and better than good as his breath brushes against my mouth, a precursor to kissing.

Toby is going to kiss me.

Super weird.

My pulse is pounding just as fast as his, and my fingers curl against his shirt.

"What are you waiting for?" I whisper, and he smiles.

"You to shove me away."

"I'll do that when you finish," I breathe.

"I shouldn't do this."

"Right." We're both breathing hard, and his arms are all the way around me now. Big, strong, flexing arms holding me tight.

He flicks his gaze up to my eyes. "God, Cara." He eases back just enough to grin at me. "You can't marry some random guy."

"Okay."

"Promise me."

"I promise..." The word fades into nothing as he lowers his head again, and this time, there's nothing brushing or light or tentative about it.

Toby is kissing me, and it's all-consuming and crazy intense. His lips are soft but insistent, demanding entrance to my mouth, and my brain totally scrambles to obey him. Sure, come on in, tongue. Oh, God, you feel good. That's new and different and panty-melting, what you're doing there. I didn't realize there were so many nerve endings in my mouth directly connected to my clit, but Toby knew.

He knows a *lot* about kissing.

He could teach classes. Masterclasses. Graduate level instruction in making out and kissing-as-foreplay. His kisses suggest all sorts of things I'm not supposed to know about Toby Hunt.

Like...he's almost certainly good at going down on a girl. That tongue makes *promises*.

And when it slides away, I chase it, because more, please. I don't ever want this kiss to end.

With a groan, he comes back, deeper and hotter, until I'm breathless and aching.

I could totally be convinced to do something seriously foolish with him right now, but he's smarter than that.

He eases his hands out of my hair, but his fingers linger on my skin, stroking my jaw. His gaze rakes over my face. "That was..."

I nod and shake my head at the same time. Yes. No. God. I rub my cheek against his thumb, soaking up one last second of contact before I set my hand against his chest and do what I promised at the start—I push him away. "That was crazy."

He gives me a rueful smile. "A mistake?"

"Definitely."

He steps back, two strides, then halts. His eyes zero in on my mouth and my heart skips a beat. Oh, boy. No good can come of that feeling.

And also, wow, this is what it feels like when someone really wants to kiss you. In this case, kiss me *again*.

Really inconvenient that the man who wants to kiss me is Ben's best friend, and a workaholic who lives on the other side of the continent from me.

But for tonight—for this single moment—I'll take it.

"It's getting dark," he finally says, stuffing his hands in his pockets.

I nod. "We should get going."

Neither of us moves at first, until he cracks a smile and turns away from me. *Come on*, his body language says. *Let's pretend we didn't just do that.*

I'm not sure I can ever forget that kiss. I take a deep breath as we start to walk. "So that's in the vault, right? Along with my underage drinking and fear of living on the Eastern Seaboard?"

"You bet."

"You know all my secrets."

He grunts quietly. "I should probably tell you more of mine, balance that out."

"Have you ever been arrested?"

He shakes his head. "No."

"But you hate New York, right?"

He looks sideways at me, his shoulders shaking with quiet laughter. "No. I mean, I love California, but I have no geography-based phobias."

"Mine isn't geography-based. It's relations-based. Meddling-based. Smothering-Nana-based."

"And yet when she says jump..."

I say how high, no matter where I am in the world. "Maybe I'll go to Australia for my next course of studies."

"Good plan, troublemaker."

Our conversation fades as we reach the street again. We stand side-by-side, silently, as he texts his driver to pull his car around to the park. It should be awkward. We *kissed*. And it was *hot*.

But it's not that weird. A little, because deep down, I want to do it again.

But on top of that is a warm, fuzzy sweetness. Toby kissed me. Because he wanted to, even though it's a terrible idea and we can't do it again.

A boy wanted to kiss me. A boy who knows how awkward

and dorky and vaguely inappropriate I am. A boy who's really a man.

A *man* kissed me.

I'd built up this whole narrative around my life where that just wouldn't happen, not in a good way. Not in a holy hotness kind of way.

"Thank you," I say quietly, bumping my arm against his.

"For losing my mind?" He laughs under his breath. "Don't thank me."

"For being a grown up about it."

"I promise you that deep down I feel like a teenage boy right now."

That pleases me, too. I grin like an idiot.

He doesn't miss my reaction. "You like that?"

"Yeah."

"Good." A dark sedan slows to a stop in front of us and Toby touches my arm. How many times has he done that before? How did I never notice how good it feels to be moved around by a guy? Especially one with big hands and strong arms. "Come on. Let's get you home. Tomorrow we fly you away from the Russo madness."

I've always been happy to come home and see my family. And happier still to get on a plane and zoom back to my own life.

For the first time, I'm left wondering if I've been running away from all the wrong things, for all the wrong reasons.

And I definitely can't marry someone who wants a green card.

Nope.

Damn Toby and his magical mouth, making the point I didn't want to hear. Marriage should be for passion.

But that doesn't solve my immediate problem of Nana and her well-intentioned but misguided threats.

I need a new plan. Plan 2.0.

Toby opens the car door for me. "Are you coming?"

I nod and hurry after him. Okay, no more thinking about that tonight, because warm fuzzy feelings. But tomorrow, in the cold light of day, I'm going to tell Toby I still need a husband. Not a real one, of course. I don't want his head to explode.

Just a temporary one.

The only solution is to resort to funny stuff, as Nana would say.

As soon as I get back to Elana's, I'm Googling how to hire an escort.

CHAPTER SEVEN

TOBY

"NO."

Cara rolls her eyes and leans back in her seat. We're halfway to Toronto, but getting nowhere with this conversation. "You're not giving the plan fair consideration."

"Because it's insane."

"Whatever. You don't even get a say."

True enough. I'm just the guy who had his tongue down her throat yesterday. What do I know about her love life, anyway?

Nothing, and it's going to stay that way. Damn it.

I slept like shit last night, replaying that kiss over and over again in my mind. Wishing I'd pulled her closer and pressed my erection into her belly. Wishing I'd dragged her back to my hotel suite instead of depositing her safely at her sister's townhouse.

Luckily today was non-stop meetings until it was time to meet Cara at the airport, so my brain was forced to take breaks from inappropriate fantasies about teaching her just how good two people can be together.

Giving up on love at twenty-four. What the bloody hell is that?

Sure, I don't really believe in love myself, but that's because I'm jaded with good reason.

Maybe Cara is, too.

No. She's too...lighthearted, too lovely.

Too innocent.

"You can't hire an escort," I grind out. "Aren't you on a student visa in Canada? Don't jeopardize that."

"I'm not going to hire a *prostitute*."

"Isn't it the same thing? You don't want to get busted for solicitation."

She stares at me like I'm an idiot. Well at least this conversation has gone a long way toward restoring our relationship to its rightful place.

No kissing. Sibling-ish mocking. Huffing and sighing and...

Jesus, she's gorgeous when she's frustrated. Pink cheeks and bright eyes.

She takes a deep breath, then gives me a level look. "Okay, let me start again from the beginning, because I think you may have missed the point of the plan."

I missed nothing. I just don't approve of her hiring some asshole to pretend to marry her, so she can tell her grandmother she eloped and ta-da, now she's married, stop worrying, Nana.

I wave for the flight attendant. If Cara's going to blithely carry on like our kiss meant nothing, I need a drink.

She's right to do so, of course. It was momentary madness.

I've learned a lot about gut calls in the last fifteen years. Learned how to lean into the bruise that fear leaves, figure out when pain is productive and when it's destructive, and walk that line carefully.

Everything about kissing Cara screamed danger, and I did it

anyway. Everything about backing off feels right—except for this one sharp spot in my chest. It feels very wrong there.

I scowl and tip back my drink as soon as it arrives. "Another," I demand roughly. I can practically feel Cara's eyebrows raise beside me, so I add a touch of nicety to the request. "Please."

Cara leans past me and smiles at the stewardess. "I'd love a glass of cranberry juice, if you have it."

Juice.

I'm guzzling whiskey and she's asking for juice.

My best friend's kid sister.

Yes, backing off is the right thing to do, that spot in my chest be damned.

And the fact that her fingers brushing against my forearm makes me halfway hard? Proof I need to get my head on straight and help Cara out, not stand in her way like some jealous wannabe boyfriend.

If there's a selfish element there, because maybe I don't mind her not dating anyone... I'm not going to examine that too closely. "Tell me the plan again," I mutter, closing my eyes.

She sighs and leans in closer. "You're the best, you know that? Okay, so I was thinking, maybe I could find a guy to play my fiancé, then my husband, just a couple of times. He'd be Canadian, of course, so when I leave Toronto, we'd regretfully decide to part ways. But it would buy me until the end of my program without Nana threatening to meddle with my grant funding."

"You know she can't really do that."

"I know, but she's a major benefactor at several Ivy League schools. What's to stop her from making a million-dollar donation to U of T and causing problems for me?"

I frown. "I could match that."

She laughs. "Okay, no. *No*. And also, the last thing we need is some crazy big-league donation battle. That would be weird."

"This whole thing is weird."

"I just want to be left alone. Is that so wrong?"

No. My chest squeezes tight. "Okay. You figure out what you need, then let me know."

I give Ben a call that night.

"Did you get my sister safely back to her dorm?"

"She lives off-campus in a condo."

"Unchaperoned?"

I laugh. "Very."

"I don't approve." He huffs a sigh. "When did she grow up?"

"Somewhere around the same time you started to feel old."

"I've been thinking about what you said, you know. About making some changes."

"Good."

"I'm officially in the market for a wife now."

It's on the tip of my tongue to tell him his entire family is crazy, but I can't break Cara's confidence. "I saw that coming a mile away. Are you going to do some sort of reality TV show to find one? Russian mail-order bride?"

"Tempting, but no. I'm going to try it the old-fashioned way, first."

Okay, so maybe he's not as crazy as his sister. "Good plan. I approve, by the way. That's the way to do it." Find someone that lights you up inside.

Bright eyes, soft lips.

"You should take your own advice," Ben says.

Probably. But I'm not going to, not any time soon. No woman can hold a candle to the only one who is completely off-limits to me.

CHAPTER EIGHT

CARA

MUCH OF THE U of T campus is picturesque and ivy-covered, but the building that houses my faculty is a tall, modern, glass-and-concrete structure. I've had three offices—all shared—in the year that I've been here, and now I'm moving into yet another. For the summer, I'll use the empty office next door to my advisor so I can help with a big research project she's just received a grant for.

And in return, she's put her name on my grant applications for the fall, although those are now in peril, thanks to my grandmother.

I shake my head. Nana doesn't really understand how my world works—although to be fair, she has more reach than most grandmothers do.

I'm just packing up the last of my things when my officemate arrives for the day. I like Helena well enough as a colleague, but our work schedules and practices never aligned, so I'm secretly happy about heading upstairs.

I'm careful not to show that, though. Nobody likes a bragger.

She gives me a polite nod, then pulls out her headphones and crawls into her work. Okay, then. Not like I was going to offer to meet up at the grad pub anyway, but...

See ya, Helena.

The usual prick of disappointment I feel after an awkward encounter like that fades when I get an unexpected text as I'm settling into my new space.

Toby: Have a good work week, troublemaker.
Cara: I'll do my best. You too!

And I do have a good work week. So busy, my plan to find a fake fiancé stalls out as my advisor's big project for me grows in scope.

Adding a pretend wedding on top of all that work would be ridiculous, I admit to myself mid-week.

So I let it slide until the Friday afternoon, when I find a white envelope in the mail slot at my apartment building. The paper is smooth and thick, and smacks of a limited run done by a high-end New York *paperie*. I don't need to look at the return address, written in flowing script, to know the letter is from Nana.

I wait until the ancient elevator has carried me up to my sixth-floor unit before opening the embossed envelope. An honest-to-God, gilded stationery piece of correspondence. This can't be good. My panic returns to the top of the To-Do-Or-Die list even before I read her careful handwriting.

Dear Cara,

I was so pleased to hear you have a change of heart about looking for love. So to that end, I've hired the services of a well-regarded Toronto matchmaker...

The letter falls out of my hand and flutters to the floor as my fingers immediately slick with sweat.

Oh, no. No, no, no...

I spin around grab for my phone. Toby's number is in my Fav List. I stab at his name, then press the phone to my ear. My hand is shaking, and that just gets worse when he doesn't answer.

Shit.

I huff out a breath and stare down at the letter. Might as well read the rest of it before totally freaking out.

Nope, too late.

I lean over and grab it.

... Toronto matchmaker. Expect a phone call from them early next week to set up an appointment. You'll need to attend a number of meetings as they pay extraordinary attention to detail so as to find you just the right man.

The right man isn't answering his phone. Also, he's off-limits. And way older than me. And Ben's best friend. *And* he lives in California...

Wait.

My heart pounds in my chest. No, Toby isn't the right man. Not for me.

But that mouth...

Well, yeah, anyone who'd been kissed like that would think they might like another taste. That's normal.

My phone rings, surprising me. I squeak and jump and die a little inside as I flop to the floor. Toby's name is flashing on the screen.

"Hi," I say as I answer it.

"What's wrong?" Oh God, he's all sleepy. His voice is warm and rough and sounds like sex.

Did I interrupt sex?

Did he call me back after I interrupted sex?

Except the sleepy... That doesn't make any sense. "Where are you?"

"Tokyo," he mumbles. "It's almost five in the morning."

"Shit. I'm sorry. I forgot."

"It's okay." His words slur together before he takes a long, slow inhale, then grunts. "I'm up. I'd have to get up in half an hour anyway, I have a breakfast meeting with Sony people."

"Fancy."

He laughs and I picture him stretching. What does he sleep in when he's traveling the world? Pajama pants that hang low on his hips? Boxer briefs? Nothing?

I suddenly want more of that picture. Not just the X-rated, Toby-is-built-like-an-Olympic-swimmer picture, but all of it. "Where are you staying?"

"The Park Hyatt. They know how I like my bacon."

"That's what you're having for breakfast?"

"Always. But they'll have these little Japanese pastries, too, and tea."

"I've had the tea there. Elana took me with her on a trip once, and we did the high tea service. And then we went to a shrine..."

"I should have brought you with me, you probably know more about being a tourist here than I do."

"How many times have you been to Japan?"

"Half a dozen at least. Always whirlwind trips."

I shake my head and smile. "That's no fun."

"This is what I'm saying. You need to teach me the way, Cara-san. Now why did you wake me up in the middle of the night?" he asks gently.

"Ah, it's...nothing. Doesn't matter."

"Is this about your need for a groom?"

"Maybe."

"I wasn't sure if you'd dropped it."

"I kinda had. And then Nana sent me a letter."

"An email?"

"No, an honest-to-God letter. Nice stationery and all."

"Sounds serious."

"She's hired a matchmaking service to find me a mate."

"Huh." His single-syllable sound is short, clipped, and hard.

"This can't happen, Toby."

"Right."

"I should just tell her to back off."

"Yes, you should. But you won't."

"I can't," I whisper.

He sighs. "Then tell her you've met a guy."

My breath catches in my throat.

"Plan 2.0," he murmurs more gently than I deserve. "Time to kick it into action. Whirlwind love affair in three, two, one..."

"What's his name? I haven't even thought of that."

"Ralph."

I snort. "No."

"Blake."

I wrinkle my nose. "No. How about Alex?"

There's a pause at his end, then he clears his throat. "Sure."

"I hope the actor I find looks like an Alex. I'm doing this all backwards."

"Actor?"

"You had a good point. I probably can't risk hiring an escort. An actor might be more money, but—"

"I'll hire the escort for you. I mean, it's important that it be someone who understands the role. An actor sounds…risky."

"I can't ask you to do that." I chew on the corner of my lip. "I probably shouldn't involve you in this at all."

"And yet here I am, waiting for the sun to rise on the other side of the globe, happily involved. Don't worry about that."

"Okay." I take a deep breath. *"I'm sorry, Nana, but I actually met a guy this week.* Sounds good?"

"Sounds great. Keep it simple. The best lies are as close to the truth as possible."

"I met him on the plane back to Toronto. He called me later in the week, and we're having coffee this weekend. I can't, in good conscience, agree to start seeing other people when he's all I can think about." I can feel my mouth curving into a smile as the story blooms to life.

"Alex sounds like a great guy," Toby says gruffly.

"Don't worry, he's going to break my heart. He'll refuse to move to Australia with me."

"And that'll be the end of that."

"Yep."

"Go call your grandmother."

"And you kick butt with your meeting with Sony."

He laughs. "They're trying to impress me, troublemaker."

"Right. I should know that, shouldn't I?"

"Nah. It's refreshing that you don't."

When we hang up, I pick up the letter again. Talking to Toby did the trick. I'm not stressed anymore. It's going to be just fine. I take a deep breath, and dial my grandmother's phone number.

CHAPTER NINE

TOBY

I LAND late Sunday night at the San Francisco airport, bone-tired and grateful to have a driver waiting to whisk me home to Palo Alto. I spend the thirty-minute drive drowsily going through my public email account.

I have a couple of private ones, too, but all of our customers know they can email me at toby@starfishinstrumentation.org and I will see it. Sometimes only whizzing by in a blur on nights like this, but I have a team of excellent customer service people who ensure that everything there gets properly responded to.

A name catches my eye and I tap the screen. Mike Rodriguez. I roll my neck as I read the message. It's apologetic in tone. He's been a customer from early on, but his latest batch of transmitters didn't pass his company's internal quality assurance check.

That's shitty, though it does happen.

But my blood runs cold as I keep reading. It's the third time it's happened in the last year, and he's afraid he needs to cancel the standing order.

Mike Rodriguez. The name is still echoing in my brain, like it should mean something more than just a disappointed customer.

I lean forward and get my driver's attention. "Sorry, Vince, change of plans." I rub the heel of my hand into my eye. "Let's stop and grab some coffee at the first opportunity. Then take me to the office instead of home."

After we hit Starbucks, I switch over to my personal messages. It's nearly three in the morning in Toronto, but I still click on her name first in my messaging app.

To my surprise, it shows her as online.

Toby: Landed at SFX. Heading to work now.
Cara: No rest for the wicked. How was your flight?
Toby: Boring. No pretty girls selling me on a long con game.
Cara: Har har har.
Toby: How goes your romantic relationship with Alex?
Cara: I've started keeping a journal about him.
Toby: What?
Cara: Okay, it's more of a log. Just so I can keep the fictional woo-ing straight.
Toby: Smart.
Cara: We had brunch today. It was lovely. And we held hands the whole way back to my place.

Here's the weird thing about jealousy. It doesn't matter if the guy is real or not. It doesn't even matter if the asshole has your middle name, not that Cara knows that.

I'm still burning up at the idea of *Alex* holding her hand and walking her home.

**Cara: I didn't make a note of whether or not he came in. Nana wouldn't ask that.
Toby: He didn't. A chaste kiss goodbye at the door.
Cara: Not that chaste. We have to like each other enough to rush to the altar.
Toby: Right. Because he's waiting for marriage.
Cara: Ooh, that's good.**

No, that's called self-preservation.

**Toby: Do you have a timeline for when you want this to happen?
Cara: Nana was surprisingly understanding. I don't think I'm in a huge rush. Maybe in a month or two? Have to let the courtship unfold.**

That will get me past the annual shareholders meeting.

**Toby: That makes sense. And shouldn't you be in bed now?
Cara: Maybe I was up late texting with Alex.
Toby: Maybe Alex should respect your need for a solid eight hours.
Cara: LOL
Cara: Good night, Toby**

CHAPTER TEN

CARA

THE NEXT WEEK FLIES BY. I spend my days listening to interviews with research subjects and comparing what I hear to the written transcripts which have been coded with qualitative data analysis. I'm looking for audio cues that change the words used, that might undercut the analysis based on text alone.

It's fascinating stuff, but repetitive after a while.

So I spend my evenings planning both my fake wedding and my fake courtship, because the former is inevitable when I'm fully in charge of the latter.

Since we're eloping, we could just go to City Hall. But that poses the logistical problem of us not actually getting married, because Alex is going to be played by some random guy Toby's going to source for me when the time comes. We can hardly get a real wedding license, and I don't think the City Hall people would be down with a fake one.

No, I'm going to have to hire a wedding officiant who is fine with performing some kind of commitment ceremony, knowing there's no paperwork, just for photographs.

Nana has no idea the hoops I'm leaping through to make her happy.

On the weekend, I take the ferry over to Toronto Island, and imagine doing it with Alex. Or Toby.

It hasn't escaped my notice that my log of Alex-related activities echoes my interactions with Toby.

Monday: Alex had to work late, but he sent me a quick text to say hi. That was sweet.

Tuesday: Tried to play it cool, because this is all new and we're just getting to know each other, but I saw a billboard that I knew would make Alex laugh, so I texted him a picture of it. He sent back a GIF of a laughing horse. I've looked at it every day since.

Wednesday: We talked on the phone tonight. Discussed weekend plans. Might go to Toronto Island.

Thursday: Looking forward to the weekend. Alex has been working non-stop on something big at work, he's distracted.

That something big is Toby's annual shareholder meeting, now just a week away. Like a lot of tech CEOs, he's also the face of his company, and this is his chance to present something new and exciting to both the shareholders and the market at large.

He hasn't talked about it much, but when he has, he's sounded worried. I want to ask him about it, but I don't want to pry, either.

It's a weird thing, shifting a relationship that has been firmly established as one thing—brother's friend, grown-up mentor—to another. A real friendship, as unexpected and weird as that sounds. But with a single, amazing kiss, Toby burst into technicolor in my life, and now I find myself wanting to talk to him every single day.

Which explains why I'm antsy on Sunday morning. I haven't heard from him since Thursday. And when he texts me, the ridiculous smile that blooms across my face is almost too much.

I don't care.

Toby: Morning. What are you up to?
Cara: Super exciting laundry.
Toby: Oh yeah?
Cara: I scored two washers right next to each other.
Toby: Your condo doesn't have laundry in it?

Ah, billionaire expectations. I'm surprised he didn't ask me why I don't just send it out to a service.

Cara: Nope.
Toby: Damn.
Cara: I like the ritual. It's fine.
Toby: Right, that makes sense.
Cara: How about you? Flying somewhere on a private jet today?
Toby: Ha. You know I don't have one of those.
Cara: Yeah. Why don't you?
Toby: I like the ritual.

Cara: LOL touché.
Toby: That's true, actually. But it's also a cost-benefit thing.
Cara: Ah.
Toby: How long will you be doing laundry.
Cara: Another hour, probably. I'm about to put everything in the dryer.
Toby: I'll call you after that?
Cara: Can't wait.

He didn't reply again, and I was left staring at that last text. Why did I say that? **Okay** or **sounds good** would have also worked. **Can't wait**. Jeez, way to sound needy, Cara.

We talk on Monday night and Tuesday at lunch, and on Wednesday, too, when he suddenly sounds excited about the shareholder meeting.

"We do this every year, and I always worry and push and stress, and then it works out just fine," he says, shaking his head ruefully at the camera. We're on video for this call, because he says he has to get a run in or he'll go mental, and when he's running, it's easier for him to have a conversation on video. So he's on a treadmill in his office in Palo Alto, and I'm sitting cross-legged on my bed in Toronto, holding my iPad and watching his t-shirt get soaked with sweat.

I am not complaining about this video request in the least. Thank heavens for light-weight cotton.

"I'll be sure to remind you of that next year," I tease.

He swipes the back of his hand across his forehead. "Thanks."

"What time is your presentation tomorrow?"

"Noon here, so mid-afternoon for you."

"I'm going to watch. No pressure."

He grins at me. "That's the good kind of pressure. I'll make sure it's extra exciting for you."

"What are you unveiling?"

"A new Bluetooth solid state memory device. I wasn't sure we'd have it working in time, but it's pretty slick."

"Fun!"

"I'll overnight you a prototype if you want to give it a whirl."

"I do." I shift my position, curling my legs up against my chest. I wrap my arms around them and rest my chin on my knees. "But you don't have to do that, of course."

"You gotta get some benefit out of being friends with the CEO."

Right. Friends.

Which means I really should end this call before he finishes his run and pulls that soaking wet t-shirt off his body. "Then I can't wait to use it."

I get another wink in response.

"Okay, you've made me feel like a total slacker. I'm going to let you go, and get in a run myself." A total lie. I'm going to end the call and flop out on my bed and replay that wink a dozen times.

He gives me a quick wave. "Talk to you later, then."

"Definitely. Break a leg tomorrow."

"It's not theater."

"It is in a way. And you're a star. You'll slay, I know it." Then I press the red button that makes him disappear, and toss my iPad aside.

Oh, Toby.

I close my eyes and stretch out. Damp t-shirt, flashing smile, dirty wink.

He hadn't meant it to be dirty, of course. But too late, my imagination was already running wild and free, looping those images backwards now. A wink, a smile, and then that t-shirt, now peeling up and off his body.

Into the shower with you, Mr. Hunt.
I'll wash your back.

CHAPTER ELEVEN

TOBY

SHAREHOLDER MEETING DAY begins before dawn with a breakfast meeting with the entire executive team. I announce quarterly bonuses that exceed their expectations, but make it clear that the supply chain problems I'm quietly seeing examples of here and there—like the Mike Rodriguez drama, which thankfully got solved quickly, but at great expense.

"We can't ever get too big to care about our first customers," I remind them.

And to prove that point, the next meeting I have is coffee with Mr. Rodriguez himself. I invited him out to California on our dime, and before we head to the hotel where the shareholder meeting will be held, I take him to our production facility.

"I know this doesn't make up for the disruption to your own work," I say as we stroll down the production line. "But we want to be transparent in our QA efforts."

"Hey, I've been in business long enough to know that bad luck sometimes strikes way more often than it should."

"Chaos theory is my nemesis," I growl.

He laughs. "Don't I know it. Listen, I know I'm just a small peanut compared to what you've achieved, but I'm seriously impressed with how you've handled this. Before you get dragged off to that hotel and all the press stuff today, I just wanted to say, thank you—again."

"You know, I didn't say this before, because I don't believe in sentimentality, but I remember your first order. It took me a while to connect the dots. But you took a chance on my processing chip when early reports were calling it glitchy. I'll never forget that."

"I've been married for thirty-five years, son. I've learned to value sentimentality. At the end of the day, the year, the decade...when you look back, it's the relationships I see. I took a chance on your company because of your heart, not your product. And as I told you, I wouldn't hesitate to go somewhere else if quality was a concern. But I knew you'd make it right, and you did. A decade from now, we'll remember this moment, too."

I have no doubt.

———

Cara: Excellent presentation. Gold star.
Toby: You watched?
Cara: I told you I would. I liked the bit about Mike Rodriguez. You've had a busy few weeks!

And the best part of it has been talking to her, which is a dangerous kind of pleasure. I need to get a handle on that feeling, because it can't rage out of control.

Toby: That's the job. Wouldn't have it any other way. But it's nice to have a weekend off.
Cara: LOL weekend off? Are you not going into the office tomorrow?

Tomorrow being Saturday.

Toby: Only for a few hours.
Cara: My face right now...

I can only imagine.

Cara: Take some time off.
Toby: Sure. Maybe we can do cyber-brunch on Sunday.
Cara: That's not helping my impression that you work too hard, but sure, I'll take it.

CHAPTER TWELVE

CARA

IT TAKES two weeks for Ben and Elana to hear I'm dating someone.

I knew they'd find out eventually. Obviously, when I fake-elope, they'd hear then at the latest.

But for some reason, I didn't really connect the dots that telling Nana to back off with her matchmaking plans would lead to my siblings being worried about this guy named Alex, and his intentions toward their baby sister.

Good thing I have my log.

I tell Ben that Alex is sweet, and a total gentleman. I'm not sure he buys it, but it's the truth, in a way.

Elana's a tougher one to divert.

"Tell me everything," she says when I answer the phone Saturday afternoon.

"Not much to tell," I hedge.

"Liar!" She sighs. "Come on, I promise I won't tell Nana and Ben. Who is this guy who's finally opened your eyes to romance?"

I hesitate. "He's...I mean...it's... Honestly, he's the last guy I ever would have thought I'd like, you know? But I knew from the second he kissed me that it was something special."

Again, not a lie. My face is flaming hot.

"When do we get to meet him?"

Whoa. "Ummm.... Not sure." I need Toby to hire him first. "He's got a lot on his plate with work right now. And you know, the whole we-live-in-a-different-country thing."

"Bring him to the Hamptons this summer."

"I might." Not. That would be way too much to ask an escort to do. Also, I'm awkward as fuck. There's no way I can pretend to be in love with some random guy for an entire weekend. We're going to do one Sunday tea with Nana before he turns out to be a workaholic who never wants to leave Toronto again.

I hear flipping on the other end of the phone. "It looks like Ben's heading to the beach house with Toby and Jake for the Fourth of July. And then again the first week of August...do either of those work? Or would you rather avoid them? What's Alex like? Would he get along with Ben's friends?"

My head swims as I imagine pretending to be in love with an escort in front of Toby. "I don't know. I said I might be able to make it, but let's not put anything down in writing..."

"There are plenty of rooms. It's really just about letting the housekeeper know how many people to shop for."

"For God's sake, Elana, I can buy my own groceries." I regret snapping at her as soon as it's out of my mouth. But seriously, how un-fun is it to schedule trips to the shore? I remember when I was a kid, and Ben would drive us down on a whim. Those weekends were the best.

"You do it your way," she says softly, and I feel even worse.

"Your way is organized. I'm sorry."

"It's fine. If you decide to visit spontaneously, it won't be that disruptive."

Story of my life. Speaking of disruptions, she still hasn't told me about the baby. I wonder if everything is okay, but if she wanted me to know, she'd tell me. "I'll come down the Fourth of July weekend. No promises about Alex. He's..." Fictional. "Private."

"Sounds good. I love you, Cara."

"Love you, too."

My brain is still spinning with that conversation on Sunday morning when Toby texts me a reminder of our cyber-brunch.

I haven't forgotten. I did a special grocery run yesterday and wrote how much I was looking forward to this in the log.

Toby: What are we having for brunch, anyway?
Cara: I've got orange juice and everything to make Eggs Benedict.
Toby: Sounds amazing. Give me forty-five minutes?
Cara: Perfect.

When he calls, it's a video call. I'm still in the kitchen, adding some garnish to my plate. I answer and pick up my plate in one hand, and my iPad in the other.

"Hey there. Just heading to my table."

"I'm still waiting for my food," he says as the picture flashes to life.

He's sitting at a table, too, but it doesn't look like his house. It looks like an empty restaurant.

I give him a confused look. "Where are you?"

"A private dining room at a country club I belong to."

"You went out for our cyber-brunch?"

"I don't know how to make Eggs Benedict myself." He says this like it makes perfect sense.

"But you could have made whatever. Toast or..."

"You're having something fancy, I wanted something similar." He grins and any thoughts I may have had about this being odd vanish.

Whatever. He wants someone else to cook for our brunch together, that's no skin off my nose.

"Besides, we're celebrating," he adds.

"Right! Your shareholder meeting went well?"

"Sure." He leans in toward the camera. "But I also got a message yesterday from Ben. Your family seems pretty stoked about Alex. Your plan is working."

I pull a face at him. "Oh. That."

"You aren't thrilled?"

"I don't know. Now that they all know, it's kind of weird." I take a deep breath. "It's getting complicated."

He laughs gently. "Yes. You knew it would."

"Right. But...it's different in reality."

"Ah." He leans back as a waiter sets a plate in front of him.

"Oh, that looks good!" I say.

"I got the smoked salmon instead of Canadian bacon."

"Hey, fun fact." I hold up my plate. "They don't even have Canadian bacon in Canada. True story. They use this delicious other kind of ham that we don't have at home, and call it back bacon. It's tasty. I'll miss it when I leave."

"We'll have to get find you an international supplier if you like it that much."

I laugh out loud before realizing he's serious. I shake my head. "I don't need special delivery of food."

"Maybe for a special occasion." He smiles, undeterred.

"Oh, Toby." I play with my food a bit as I try to find a polite way to say I don't like to be spoiled. Which is, in and of itself, an incredibly lucky thing to be able to say. "I really appreciate the thought. But the thing is, within reason, I don't like to take advantage of..."

"My wealth?" Where Elana might bristle, Toby just shrugs. "I get that. I don't like to waste money, either—not owning a private jet being just one example of that. But if you ever got homesick for something you'd had in one of your many temporary homes, I'd move mountains to get it for you."

His words are earnest, but there's a roughness to them, too, one that slices under my skin. I should push back against it, tell him I don't need that kind of dedication—I don't want it—but that wouldn't be true.

So instead I change the subject, because while I can't lie, I can evade like a champ. "Speaking of extravagance, Elana says you're coming to the Hamptons a couple of times this summer."

"That's the plan. I love the Russo beach house."

"She wants me to bring Alex."

He chokes on the bite of food he'd just put in his mouth. "Excuse me?"

"Right? These are the kind of details I didn't think through before leaping into my crazy plan."

He covers his mouth as he swallows, then waves his hand as if that's a minor detail. "So the guy works a lot and can't get to the shore."

"That's what I told her."

He winks. "Great minds."

"This is your chance to tell me this is just too crazy."

He gives me a long, studied look, then shakes his head. "I like your brand of crazy."

"You're the only one."

"Ben and Elana love you."

"I know. And Nana does, too. But there's a difference between love and like. And none of them *get* me, so how can they *like* me?"

"Well, I get you. And I think you're doing what you've gotta do. Don't overthink it. You'll have a quickie fake wedding, a quickie fake annulment, and buy yourself a few more months of... okay this plan is crazy." He set his elbows on the table and leans in toward the camera. "Jesus, Cara, just tell your grandmother the truth."

"No."

"The risk analysis is terrible."

"Don't bring your business acumen to this conversation, Toby Hunt. That's not what I like about you." I'm lying. I like everything about him. "Come on. We've been over this. There's zero chance I'm actually going to get married any time soon. That would require dating, which isn't on my agenda in any way, shape, or form."

He doesn't say anything for a long, agonizing set of beats. It feels like a minute, at least, and a minute of silence is a long freaking time. "So if this isn't a business plan, then what is it?" he finally asks.

"I just want... to be normal, in my Nana's eyes. For a while. And yeah, the fake marriage isn't going to work out, but that will be my fake husband's fault. I'll have given it a go."

"A fake go."

"Yeah." God, it sounds pathetic, and a weird ache swells inside me. I blink hard, desperate not to ruin our cyber-brunch with tears.

I have never wanted my sister's insane life. A husband with a crazy job, four boys under the age of ten. A career of her own. A constantly revolving set of household staff to support their crazy home life.

My parents had a weird marriage, too. And now they're

divorced and re-married, my father three times over. Nana had hated that so much, she'd cut him out of the company.

I sigh heavily. Well, my fake divorce is likely to cure her of wanting me on the board.

"Cara?"

I snap my attention back to the iPad on the table. "I drifted there."

"Are you okay?"

"Totally fine. Now that you're done with the shareholder meeting, what's next for Starfish Instrumentation?"

The question is forced, and far too bright, but Toby accepts yet another change of subject from me. "Bah. You don't want to hear about that."

I pick up my fork and stab at my breakfast. "No, I really do." I take a deep breath and give him a smile as I lift my gaze back up. "There's nothing I'd rather talk about right now."

CHAPTER THIRTEEN

TOBY

I'M in our production lab the following weekend when Cara texts me. She's gone to New York to have tea with her grandmother, their monthly ritual.

**Cara: Nana asked me if I could see Alex being the one.
Toby: What did you say?
Cara: I asked her if she meant the first of many, and she laughed.
Toby: That's not an answer.
Cara: I know.**

He's not real. It doesn't matter what she tells her grandmother. He's a figment of her imagination, a prop to keep her independence.

But she still hasn't asked me to hire an escort to play him for a staged wedding.

I start to message her back that maybe she can buy some time with casual dating, when she sends the text I've been dreading for weeks now.

Cara: Now she's talking about the matchmaking service again. Time to get serious. What do you need from me for the escort?

I take a deep breath and remind myself this doesn't matter, it's not the end of the world.

Toby: Time, date, place. An email address you don't mind him using to coordinate further with you.
Cara: Okay. I'll let you know once I'm home again.
Cara: Thank you. You're the best.

Hardly.

I slam my fist down on the steel work bench before I remember I'm holding my phone. The sharp crunch of glass is a fitting coda to a conversation I *knew* I was going to have at some point.

What did you think your free little bird was going to do, fly back to Palo Alto again?

She wants to live her life. Move to Australia. Have nothing to do with men or business or family...

She wants nothing to do with me beyond our growing friendship.

I need some fucking perspective.

I need to help her out, exactly as she's asked me to, and get over my ridiculous, possessive affection for her.

I stalk out of the lab and across the bright atrium-style

walkway to the executive offices. My assistant is at his desk, his new puppy at his feet.

"I need a new phone," I tell him. "And then you should go home because life is short."

He raises one eyebrow at me. "What exactly happened in the lab? Did you discover the secret to work-life balance?"

Something like that. Instead of an answer, I hand him my phone, the cracked screen mocking me silently from where he sets it on his desk. Everything syncs to our cloud storage. I've lost or damaged enough phones to know it really can only be a SIM-card transportation device.

By the time I'm settled behind my desk, he's in front of me, holding out a brand-new phone. No cracks, no sign I lost my temper.

"Thank you."

"That was the last one I had in my desk. Don't break this one until Monday."

I give him a tight, acknowledging smile. "I'll do my best. Now go home."

I spend the next hour poking around the internet, trying to figure out the best way to safely hire an escort I'd trust with Cara, before I give up and call my friends.

Ben doesn't answer, so I try Jake next.

He's busy, too.

It's for the best. When they ask why I want to hire an escort, I won't be able to tell them.

No, I'm on my own with this.

I take a deep breath and go back to Google.

CHAPTER FOURTEEN

CARA

DATE, time, and place.

The three words rocket around in my mind for a few days. The narrative around Alex was easy at first, logging dates with him that mirrored phone calls with Toby. But now the fantasy is diverging from reality and I can't crib my notes from real life.

Well, an elopement could happen quickly. Time to rip the bandage off.

I should be done with this current project for my advisor by the end of the week, and then the following week is pretty light.

Perfect time to get hitched.

I'll need some proof. Would I hire a photographer if I were doing this for real?

I think so.

I send a few inquiries out, to both photographers and officiants. Three officiants turn me down because we won't have a license, but one says yes, and he's wide open Tuesday through Friday.

Two photographers also get back to me. One can only do

Monday, but the other is available all week in the middle of the day.

Taking a deep breath, I call Toby. He answers right away.

"Can you find me someone for next week? Any day, Tuesday through Friday, between the hours of ten and three. I'd need him for two hours, I think. A quick service and some photographs. And then I'd like him to be available for a trip to New York City..." My voice wobbles and steel my nerves. *Pull your shit together, Cara.* "For the last weekend in June. Leaving New York on the second of July."

He repeats some of that. I can hear him writing it down. Then he pauses. "You won't bring him to the shore for the Fourth?"

"No." A weird, squirmy shame rushes through me. "I couldn't do that long. Really just twenty-four hours. Fly in, stay at a hotel, visit Nana, fly back again. So he'll need a passport."

"Got it."

"So the plan is—"

Toby cuts me off. "Cara, maybe wait until he emails you."

"Of course."

"It's just—"

"No, that makes sense." I look at the clock. "And it's the middle of your work day. I'll let you go."

"I'll text you later." But he already sounds distant, and that's for the best.

I can't get too attached to him. He has an empire to run and I have my own life to live—the reason I started this entire ruse in the first place.

To that end, I pack up my computer into my messenger bag. But instead of heading for the subway station to cut across the top of downtown to my apartment building, I set out along Bloor Street, then cut north into Yorkdale so I can hit the Whole Foods.

I usually skip around the shopping mall, especially when the weather is nice, but something draws me into Yorkdale Village this afternoon.

Well, not something. I know exactly what I'm looking for as soon as I pull open the door.

I'm looking for a dress.

What am I going to write in the log tonight?

Alex said... "Even though you're not leaving for a year, I'm already sad about saying goodbye."

"It doesn't need to be goodbye. No matter where I go next, we'll have phone calls and video chat. We can do cyber-brunch whenever we want."

"I like real brunch."

"Me, too."

"You know, I was thinking...if we were married, you could stay."

I'm not planning on staying. But there's something about his face, his earnest expression, that makes me want to consider putting down roots for the first time. Maybe. Probably not.

"What do you think? Want to get married?"

As far as proposals go, it's not that impressive. For some reason I don't quite understand, I still say yes.

The end of the story needs some romantic massaging, but I've got time to work on it. Maybe we had the conversation whispered in the hallway at my building on campus, him leaning over me, one hand plastered against the wall, his lips brushing my ear...

That's better.

And then he had to go back to work, because he's always busy, and so I came here to find a dress.

Right.

What kind of dress do I want after that kind of proposal?

I slow down and cast my attention into the first store on my left, then the next. Sporty, funky...no, nothing like that. I should be humming with excitement. I want to remember this day, this private moment, for the rest of my life.

I cross to the other side and poke my head into a store there. Lots of tulle, promising. But everything is a bit fussy for the locations I've narrowed this down to. I think I'm going to get hitched on campus, because as Toby would say, that's been my home here in this city.

That means some walking, depending where we want to do it. So the dress needs to be soft and light.

I keep hunting. Four more stores, four more nopes.

But the last shop at the end is perfect.

Three dresses leap into my arms, and I'm practically skipping as I head toward the change room.

None of them are designed to be wedding dresses, of course. I'm not going to go that far with this charade. The first one is short, the hem brushing my knees. It's soft and floaty, with a bit more fabric in the back. Very romantic, and from a distance, anyone would think I was just on a date with my...Alex. My escort.

The second is pretty, but too pretty, really. It's covered in glittery bits, some rhinestones and sequins here and there, and if we were eloping at night, maybe. Not for a daytime thing, though.

I giggle to myself as a perfect nighttime elopement springs fully formed into my head. I've been reading too much about weddings lately.

The last one is the longest, the chiffon skirt falling all the way to the ground. It's the palest shade of blue I've ever seen, and even before I contort myself to zip up the snug, strapless bodice, I know it fits me like a glove.

It might not be the right dress to wear. The first one would suffice. I carefully unzip—after twirling twice—and then stand back so I can look at them both.

My heart is already set on the pale blue one. It looks like a sexy, modern version of Cinderella's dress, if Cinderella liked her dresses strapless and so tight she didn't need a bra.

Toby looks like Prince Charming...

And that's reason enough for me to also buy the shorter yellow dress. There's no way I'm getting fake-married in a dress that makes me fantasize about Mr. Right-If-He-Wasn't-Totally-Off-Limits.

CHAPTER FIFTEEN

TOBY

IT TAKES me a few hours to set up a secure email for Cara to communicate with "Alex". The task itself takes two minutes. The worrying beforehand about whether or not it's the right thing to do is what takes too damn long.

But when I pull the trigger and send her the details, I don't feel the expected rush of regret. The truth is, there is no alternative. I can't call her up and tell her I want to date her instead, that I can protect her from Nana's meddling.

She deserves more than being tethered to a boyfriend on the other side of the continent. She deserves to be free, and this gets her that.

It doesn't feel quite right, but it doesn't feel as wrong as I expected, either.

I take a quick look at my calendar. I have a Q&A with the customer service team tonight. We're ordering in dinner for the day shift to stay late, and the overnight crew to come in early.

But I've got two hours until then, and Cara should be home from work by now.

I use the controls on my desk to lock my office door and activate the privacy screen built into the glass walls.

Toby: Sent you an email with the contact information for your Alex. He prefers later in the week, Thursday or Friday.
Cara: Awesome. I'll pick Friday, it's most realistic. And…
Toby: What?
Cara: You're going to laugh.
Toby: Try me.
Cara: I bought a wedding dress today.

I flex my fingers. No, I'm not laughing. That tight squeeze in my chest isn't humor.

I tap on her name and hit the call button. I find it easier to dig into enthusiasm when I can hear her voice.

"Is that totally silly?" she asks when she answers. She sounds out of breath.

"Not at all. Where are you?"

"Just got home. Had to carry the dresses up the stairs because there's a guy working on the elevator. Six floors trumps my half-hearted step class ability."

I chuckle. "Dresses, plural?"

"I bought two. It's a long story."

"I want to hear it."

She tells me about walking through the mall, trying to get in the right head space, then finding the dresses, and the nighttime dress she put back. By the time she's finished, I actually am excited for her. Weird as this plan may be, she's having quite the adventure.

"Do you want to see them?" she asks in a breathy rush. "Or not. Maybe not."

"I do," I say before I can stop myself.

"I'll text you some pictures."

"Or we could switch to video..."

"Yeah?" Man, the eagerness in her voice is addictive. Whenever she decides she's ready to find a real boyfriend to share her life with, he's going to be the luckiest fuck in the world.

My phone chirps with the request to initiate a video connection, and I accept. Her grinning face pixels into view. "Hey there," I say, leaning back in my chair.

"Look at the big fancy CEO, wearing a suit and tie," she teases.

I grin. "I like suits. And I've got a thing tonight. Gotta look like the boss."

"You're not one of those guys who prefers to work in jeans and a tee?"

"Those are good, too."

She pulls her knee up into view. "And I'm in yoga pants."

"I'm definitely not going to complain about that," I say without thinking.

She blushes.

I should try to walk that back.

I don't. "So... dresses?"

She shifts her phone so I can see more of her apartment behind her. She's in her living room, which I've never seen before. The last time we did a video call, she was in her bedroom.

It's a small space, and she doesn't have a ton of furniture. A couch, a coffee table covered in books, and beyond that, a patio door. Hanging from the curtain rod are two garment bags.

"Hang on..." She scrambles away from the camera. "Can you see me?"

"Yep." But as I say that, her phone falls over. There's a scramble, then I see her face again as she picks it up.

"Sorry about that. I don't have a great place to prop you up in here. Maybe I'll put you..." She walks a few paces, then sets me down again. "There. You're on my bookshelf now."

This view is a different angle of her living room, and a hallway leading to what I assume is her bedroom and bathroom. "Cozy place."

She shrugs as she steps back. "It's all I need."

"I like it. It's nicer than the studio I had in Boston."

"Weren't you and Jake roommates?"

"The first year, on campus. After that, I moved into my own place. I can be a night owl, especially when I'm working on a project. Although now I mostly just approve the work other engineers do."

"Do you miss the hands-on stuff?"

"Every day." Another thing I didn't mean to say.

"That's..." She bites her lower lip. "I don't know. How is that for you?"

I rub my jaw. "It's fine. You can't have it all. I also love running this company and bringing new technology to millions of people. Toby the Engineer is replaceable. Toby the CEO...less so."

"As long as you're happy." She winks at me. "Okay, now I need Toby the Fashion Expert."

"I'm definitely not that."

"Well, you're the closest thing I've got to a best friend," she tosses over her shoulder as she moves out of sight. "So suck it up, buttercup. Time for a fashion show." She pops back into view holding one of the garment bags. "I'll try this on and be right back. Do CEO things for two minutes."

I watch her disappear into her bedroom and push the door shut, then I minimize the video window on my phone so I can synch it to my computer monitor. If I'm going to be asked for real advice, I want to see her on a—

Big screen.

As the video pops onto my twenty-seven-inch monitor, I realize her bedroom door didn't close all the way.

I can't see much, just her bare arm and a hip, the outer curve of her bare leg.

My mouth goes dry.

"Hey, Cara..." I don't say it loud enough for her to hear me from the other room, though. I close my eyes, because she didn't invite me to see her like this, and I'm a gentleman.

But then I open them again, because it's just her arm.

A hip.

The long, bare stretch of a leg.

The rest I fill in from my very vivid imagination, and it's glorious. I'm a gentleman, but I'm not a saint.

She's out of view completely now, and I can hear her talking to herself as she sorts the first dress out. "This one might need a bra... Damn it. Where is my strapless... Oh, fuck it, I'll go without."

That should probably be filed under too much information, but my dick does not agree. He is more than willing to provide fashion commentary on how the dress looks with or without a bra.

He is an animal.

I close my eyes again.

"Okay," she says, her voice louder, and I open my eyes.

"Wow." I sit up straight and lean forward, taking in the knee-length cocktail dress. It's a warm yellow, floaty and perfect. She looks like sunshine and happiness in it. "That's gorgeous."

And she doesn't need a bra in it. My pants get tighter at the slight sway of her breasts beneath the fabric.

She does a little twirl. "It's nice, isn't it?"

"Very."

She stops and frowns at me. "You changed your camera."

"I did. I put you on my computer with the push of a button. We've got an app for that."

"Fun." She grins. "Busy doing CEO stuff while I changed?"

Like imagining her naked? "Yeah. Always gotta multi-task."

She spreads her arms wide. "Okay, so this is option one." She holds up her index finger. "Be right back."

She dashes into her room, and again the door doesn't close all the way.

Again, I stare at that space and hate myself for how hard I get at the glimpses of her body.

This time, I'm watching when she pokes her head out of her room and looks toward the camera. I see the nervous moment of hesitation, then the way she draws on an inner strength and pushes herself into the hallway.

"Show me," I growl, and she gives a shy smile as she swishes her way toward me.

This dress is on a whole other level. It's sexy and magical, with a tight, fitted bodice covered in an overlay of some sort, then an endlessly long skirt that billows and flows as she walks, revealing a teasing slit up one side.

More leg to drive me wild.

When she stops in front of the camera, it's like she's at the end of a catwalk, arms akimbo and her face a fierce mask.

"You like this one best," I say confidently.

She lifts her chin. "Yes."

"I do, too."

That's what she wanted to hear—and it's the truth.

She beams at me, then ducks her head.

"What is it?"

"I didn't know if it was too much. If I could pull it off. It's so..."

Sexy. It's the sexiest dress I've ever seen in my life. Or maybe that's just because Cara is in it.

"It's a bit out there. A statement, maybe. And I realized... this is the type of dress I'd pick to actually get married in, you know? I worry I'm wasting it on a mock event."

"Ah."

"I mean, nobody would ever...and if I ever did get married for real, it wouldn't be anything like what I've planned, and this wouldn't really be an appropriate dress anyway. But if I had my way..."

"Why wouldn't your real wedding be what you want?"

She wrinkles her nose. "An afternoon elopement on campus? That's not the Russo way. Can you imagine Elana missing an opportunity to put five little boys in matching tuxedos? If I ever get married for real, it'll be...lunch at The Plaza. Or a weekend in the Hamptons."

"Even if it's not what you want?"

She gives me a solemn look. "They'd never know it wasn't."

"I'd know."

She takes a deep breath. "Well, that's not a concern for now, anyway."

"Wear that dress. It's perfect."

"You think?"

"Yes. Definitely."

She turns away, heading back to her room.

"Make sure you close your door all the way," I say gruffly.

She shoots a quick glance over her shoulder, then holds my gaze as she realizes what I mean, her eyes wide and her mouth curved in a knowing smile. "Toby Hunt, did you watch me get changed?"

"I just saw your arm." And hip. And leg. A lot of leg, but I don't feel I need to be that specific.

"I don't mind," she says, her eyes brightening. She stands

there, still for a second or two, then she reaches behind her. "If you were here, I'd probably tease you now and ask you to unzip me."

"If you did, I'd use it as an excuse to kiss you again."

She gasps. It's quiet, but I hear it as she turns her head back to center.

I can't see her face.

That was the wrong fucking thing to say.

Fucking hell. I open my mouth, ready to apologize for thinking with my dick, but the words die before they can form, because she slowly begins to unzip her dress.

The zipper starts in the middle of her back.

She takes her time, and slowly the dress peels apart, revealing an ever-growing slice of bare skin.

Maybe the zipper never ends.

Maybe I might swallow my tongue.

So many possibilities.

I don't dare lean forward. I don't even breathe.

She stops when her hand reaches the curve of her bottom, and as the fabric gapes above her fist, I see unexpected black ink on her skin.

Cara has a tattoo.

"I didn't know if it was too much. If I could pull it off. It's so..."

She's a gorgeous contradiction. Unaware of the strength of her own sex appeal, but so desperate to embrace it anyway. A quiet girl with a sexy tattoo. A rebel who refuses to date under the pretense that nobody is good enough for her, when really I think she worries she's not good enough herself.

She's perfect.

And not because of a tattoo, or a dress, although those are both causing my blood supply to do some serious re-routing right now.

She straightens her spine, then holds her bodice to her chest with one hand and picks up her skirt with the other. "Good night, Toby," she calls as she heads into her room.

"Night," I say under my breath. I disconnect the call, then sit quietly in my office for a few minutes.

Thinking.

Worrying, too.

My assistant pings me ten minutes before the Q&A, and I drag my mind back to work. It takes more effort than I'd like to admit.

Most of my brainpower is still stuck on how many kisses it would take to trail from the nape of her neck, down her spine, to edges of that tattoo.

And what Cara will say when—when, and not if—I tell her I want to.

CHAPTER SIXTEEN

CARA

WHEN I GO BACK to my phone—fully clothed in my usual yoga pants and t-shirt—Toby is long gone.

My pulse is still racing from that exchange.

Friends can flirt, right?

And that's all that was. But whoa, it was fun.

Maybe it was the dress.

I'm definitely wearing it for the elopement if it gives me magical acting skills.

But kissing Toby in the park was the same. No awkwardness, just easy, sexy teasing, and that's a dangerous train of thought.

I check my email, and sure enough, there's a message from Toby introducing me to Alex. He's got a disposable email address, presumably to keep me out of escort-hiring-jail. Not like that's a real thing, except in Toby's mind, but I appreciate the concern.

From: Cara Russo

To: Alex
Subject: Friday, June 23 details

Thank you for helping me with this...project. The first date is Friday, June 23. We'll need to discuss a trip to New York after that, but that timing is flexible based on your availability. Alex is a workaholic—ha!

On Friday, I've hired a photographer and an officiant.

We'll meet the photographer on the platform of St. George Station at eleven, take a few photos there, then head onto campus. I have a permit organized, so this is all allowed, and that's where the officiant will be meeting us. As a reminder, they don't know you're an...actor. The photographer thinks this is an actual wedding, and the officiant knows we don't have a license and we just want a commitment ceremony.

Do you have any questions? If it's easier, we can text using the email app.

Nice to "meet" you,
Cara

He doesn't reply before I go to sleep.

But when I wake up in the morning, there's a new contact in my messaging app. Again, just Alex.

Alex: Nice to meet you, too. I do have a couple of questions.
Cara: Hi! Shoot.

Alex: How will I know who you are?
Cara: I've lived here for a year; I've never seen a bride on the subway in that time.
Alex: LOL Good point. How will you know who I am?

I think about that for a second. Oh, I can give him the flowers assignment. I haven't gotten around to that yet.

Cara: How about you get the flowers? You'll be wearing an orchid on your suit jacket, and you'll have a small bouquet for me, too. That's how I'll know you're my fiancé. I'll look for the flowers.
Alex: Sure, I can do that.
Cara: You can add that to the acting bill.
Alex: Don't worry about that. Next question: Is there any backstory I need to know for why we don't have a license?
Cara: I stuck to the truth as close as I could. We don't philosophically believe in marriage, but our families want us to get hitched. The photos are mostly for them.
Alex: And a little bit for you?

Oh, perceptive. I find myself laughing and smiling as we text.

Cara: Well I do like my dress.
Alex: This sounds like a fun adventure.
Cara: It's turning into that, yes. Thank you again for your assistance.

Alex: That's my job.

Of course it is. Right. I keep my last reply short and to the point.

Cara: Okay, I'll see you next Friday! Eleven in the morning on the platform of St. George Station. I'll be the bride in blue.

———

"I've been thinking about something you said last week," Toby says, his voice low and quiet in my ear.

I'm curled up on my bed. I called him almost an hour ago, and we've been talking about nothing and everything, except for what's going to happen tomorrow.

"What did I say?"

"You don't think you'll ever get married."

"Yeah." I pick at the blanket. That's getting dangerously close to the topic we've been avoiding.

"This plan of yours...it all hinges on Alex breaking up with you."

"Or me breaking up with him. It doesn't really matter."

"But the relationship will end when you leave Toronto."

"Yes."

"What if Alex didn't refuse to leave Toronto? What if he'd follow you?"

"Alex isn't real."

"I know."

"So I don't understand the question."

"You're hell bent on assuming that no guy will ever want to

follow you around the globe, or maybe even share your wanderlust."

Nobody I want, anyway. "Are you saying my standards are too high?"

"No, they're perfect. Don't settle for anything less than a mate who will follow you to the ends of the earth." He says it the same way the rest of the conversation has gone, slow and smooth, but the little hairs on my back of neck lift.

I've never allowed myself to want that before, to think that was possible for me. But if Toby can see it, maybe one day...

I stretch out, pressing myself deeper into the pillows. "That's some excellent advice...do you ever believe it for yourself?"

He laughs quietly. "Sure. I want all sorts of things. A family. Dorky domestic stuff like going to a farmer's market and cooking dinner together. Arguments over throw cushions. That kind of thing sounds awesome. But I'll never get there if I can't find someone who understands the unique push and pull of my career."

CHAPTER SEVENTEEN

TOBY

CARA HESITATES BEFORE SHE REPLIES. "I want you to find happiness, too."

I already have. I don't know why I said that shit about family and furniture. It's true, but it's not what I need to be filling her head with right now.

One thing at a time.

She lets out a little yawn. "I should get to sleep. I'm getting married tomorrow, after all."

"Not for real."

"No, but it still feels…"

Wrong. Hasty. Misguided. I want to finish that sentence for her in a dozen discouraging ways, but that's not what she needs. "How does it feel?"

"Disquieting."

That's a better word than I could have come up with, anyway. "Ah, my troublemaker."

"What's the weather like there?" she asks abruptly.

I check the app on my home screen. "Low seventies. Nice."

"It just started raining here. Storm is coming in."

I stop unpacking my suitcase and listen carefully. I'm grateful for having a suite big enough that I'm not anywhere near a window, so she can't hear that it's on my end, too. "Do you like the rain?"

"Love it. I've got my windows open."

"Then you should go to sleep, listening to the rain."

"I will." She doesn't hang up, though. "Can I tell you a secret?"

"Of course."

"Promise not to read too much into it?"

"I promise."

"I can't stop thinking about our kiss," she whispers. "How if things were different, it might have been the start of something."

I fold myself into the armchair in the corner and lean back, closing my eyes as she talks. I picture the words sliding over her lips.

Don't think about her mouth.

Too late.

"Why did even we stop kissing? That was a mistake. You could have taken me back to your hotel that night, you know. We could have done so much more..."

I swallow hard. If I say something, if I push the conversation where I want it to go, she might stop me. If I say something, *I* might stop me. The spell might snap and I'd realize how stupid an idea this is.

You know how stupid—

I turn off my brain because thinking is definitely going to ruin this moment. "That's exactly what would have happened, too. I'd have done everything to you that night. Kissed every last inch of your body and made you scream my name."

If I thought that would shock her, I underestimated her. She makes a soft, sweet sound of acquiescence instead. "Yes..."

One word. All I needed to hear, and my blood is pounding. This isn't how I was going to do this. Tomorrow, I'm going to show her everything in my heart that I've foolishly held back.

Tonight, though, I can share other secrets I've kept from her. Every dirty desire she's enflamed, every secret fantasy I hope to play out together.

"You'll let me do that, won't you? Sometime soon?" I work at my buttons, opening my shirt. I'll get to my dress pants in a minute. They're fucking tight already, but I can't take myself in hand until I know she's there with me. If we're doing this, we're doing it together. "We'll steal away somewhere. An anonymous hotel suite with a king-sized bed for me to lay you out on."

"Anywhere."

"Australia."

She laughs gently. "Maybe we can hook up somewhere closer than that. At first."

My heart leaps, and my dick throbs. Sex more than once. It's as romantic as we get maybe, but I'll take it. "Work our way through the continents. It's going to take me some time to learn all the things you like."

"I'll like everything with you." Her voice catches, and I push myself out of the chair.

So damn close to telling her I'm down the road. To inviting myself over and blowing the entire thing.

I don't want her to be lonely, or sad, or have any doubt. Whatever caused that hitch in her voice, I want it gone.

I want to shield her from everything in the world, and I know that's not possible.

No, tonight I have one task. Distract her from tomorrow. I prowl toward the bedroom and fling my tie against the white bedding. "I'll want a chance to unzip you out of a dress."

"Can I undress you, too?"

"I've already started."

"Slow down..." She drags in a breath. "Let me help you with your shirt. Are you wearing a suit?"

"I am. Tie's off."

"I've thought about your chest and back so many times, it's embarrassing."

"Never. Tell me more."

"When I woke you up in Tokyo. I wondered what you were wearing."

"Boxer briefs." Her happy sigh makes me groan. "What are you wearing now?"

"A t-shirt and..."

"And?"

"Panties." She whispers the word, which makes it that much dirtier.

I swallow hard. "Take those off."

"But you're still dressed."

I shrug out of my shirt. It flutters to the floor. "I'm getting there. You just pushed my shirt to the ground."

"And you just peeled my underwear down my legs." Her words rush out on a single breath.

I groan. "I have a lot of fantasies about your legs, you know that?"

"No. Really?"

"Fuck. Cara, I want your legs wrapped around my head. I want to press them wide open as I push into you, and feel them tight around my hips as I make you mine."

She whispers my name, and it's all the encouragement I need.

"Touch yourself. I want you to fall asleep with my name on your lips, after I've worked you up and wrung you out. I want you on your knees, in my arms, under my tongue. I want to taste every last inch of you. Feel every last inch of you."

I stretch out on the bed and unzip my pants.

"You with me?"

"Yes."

"I'm stroking myself. I'm so hard for you."

"Seriously?"

I laugh, even though it's strained. "Serious as a heart attack."

"Toby is this...okay?"

Fuck. "So okay, gorgeous. Really. If you want to..."

"I want to. I need this tonight."

That's a stab in the heart. If she doesn't need this tomorrow, too, I'll have ruined everything. The only thing I can do is show her that I'm right there with her. "Me, too. I've wanted you for weeks."

"I don't have a lot of experience."

I tip my head back. "We'll figure out what we like together."

"Tell me again that you're hard."

"Like a rock. It hurts so good when I stroke myself."

"I want to do that. Touch you."

"Yes. Your fingers. Fuck." I squeeze my cock at the base and imagine her exploring me. Tentative, then more sure. "You can touch me anywhere you want."

"If I'm stroking you, what are you doing?"

"Squeezing you close. I want to get my hands on your hips, your ass. My mouth on your lips, your neck, your breasts. I want to make you squirm, then stroke between your legs and make sure you're wet for me."

"I am..."

"I need to taste you there, too."

"Oh. Please. Yes." Her sighs are coming faster now, shakier. Good. I'm going to make her come like this, with the ghost of a fantasy about me going down on her.

I'll save being inside her for the real deal.

"Tell me how you're touching yourself, Cara. Do you rub your clit or dip your pretty fingers inside?"

"I rub." Her words catch, and that little break makes my balls draw tight.

"Your fingers are mine. Circling, faster and faster. Your clit's getting hard, isn't it? Hard and needy. I want that on my tongue. I want to feel you throb for me."

"It is. Oh, I'm..." She gasps, a sexy little sound that goes on and on. I roll my thumb over my crown, wet with pre-come, and listen to the glorious noises she makes as she shatters, then slowly comes back to me. Each utterance jacks up my need to join her.

"Oh, Toby," she breathes, and I come undone. With a strangled shout, I jerk my cock, pointing it toward my belly as my come spurts hot against my skin.

Well, hell.

I bite my lip to keep from saying the uncensored emotions barreling through me.

"That was..." She giggles. "Hot. Right?"

"Crazy hot." I swallow all the other words. "Now go to sleep."

"I'm going," she says drowsily.

"Sweet dreams, troublemaker."

But that title really belongs to me now. And she has no idea.

CHAPTER EIGHTEEN

CARA

I'M SINKING into yet another dream about Toby's fingers when I realize the sun is pretty warm on my face for the early morning.

With a gasp, I jolt upright in bed. Where the hell is my phone? It's definitely not breakfast time. The sunlight streaming through the window is mid-morning light.

Mid-morning.

Fuckity fuckers, I'm late.

I throw the blankets off my bed.

Still no sign of my phone. Last night, I was talking to Toby… oh *God*, the phone sex.

Okay, I'll freak out about that later. And then…

From under my bed, I hear a muted chime. I leap out of bed and slip on a sock, jamming my toe against the nightstand as I twist and drop to the floor.

First time in my life I've ever tried a ninja move like that. Last time, too. Dorks aren't meant to leap out of bed, ready for action.

I'm not ready for anything.
Action, a fake wedding, responding to...
Toby's six text messages.
Oh. Sweet. Mercy.

I wince as I sit down on the floor and lean back against the bed frame. I swipe in to my phone. But his texts aren't about last night.

Toby: Morning. Remember, you look stunning in that dress.
Toby: You up? Break a leg today.
Toby: Cara?
Toby: Either you've slept in, or you've got cold feet.
Toby: That's okay if you do.
Toby: Should I be worried?

Oh God. I quickly reply to the last one, then add a belated greeting.

Cara: NO!
Cara: Morning.

I blink the sleep out of my eye and focus on the clock in the corner of my phone screen. Quarter after nine. I have an hour and forty-five minutes before I need to be two subway stops away.

I've got this. It'll be fine.

Cara: Slept in. Yes. Fine. Shower now.
Toby: LOL okay

Toby in a nutshell. I'm freaking out, he's cool as a cucumber.

I need coffee first. Good coffee, and fast. I throw on shoes and grab my wallet. In the hallway, I find a neighbor who I don't know waiting for the elevator.

He gives me an absent smile. "Been waiting a few minutes," he says.

Oh no.

I head for the stairs. We'll call the jog down them further ninja training. For today is the first day of the rest of my bad-ass life, or something like that.

In the lobby, I see a sign on the elevator door.

Out of Service

Would have been nice if they'd put one of those on each floor to let us know. I run outside and down the block to the coffee shop there, only to find another sign, this one more formal.

A Toronto Public Health closure notice, framed in no-go red.

CLOSED

Okay, Universe. I get it. This is karma for trying to trick Nana.

But my *coffee shop*, too? How many times have I grabbed a latte here? Am I lucky I'm still alive?

My stomach twists. I could go two more blocks to Starbucks, but the lineup will be insane, and I'm already eating into my shower time.

I trudge back to my building, and up the six flights to my floor again.

Neighbor guy is still standing in front of the elevator.

"It's out of service," I mutter before letting myself into my apartment.

Cara: Went for coffee before my shower, and my favorite place is closed because of an unclean kitchen. And the elevator here is busted. This is a bad sign, right?
Toby: It'll be fine.
Cara: What are you doing up so early? Did you know I'd need a pep talk?
Toby: Something like that.

I send him a heart emoticon before heading into the bathroom to get pretty before my next freak-out.

It comes as I slide my Metropass through the reader in the Bloor/Yonge station. The turnstile beeps and I push through, but I immediately regret it. In front of me are two teenagers giving me a what-the-crap-are-you-wearing-lady look, and behind me there's a big crowd, shoving me forward.

I twist away from everyone, angling toward the wall. First I tuck my TTC card away, then I pull out my phone.

My fingers shake as I open an email window and begin to type in the name Alex. It auto-fills with his email address.

I huff out a breath and try to figure out what to say. *Sorry, couldn't get on the train. Best of luck with your next escort gig. I'll pay you extra for the trouble of being stood up.*

But I don't have a signal. I move backwards, trying to find the faint connection that's sometimes on the platform. Nothing.

With a squeal, the train pulls into the station and the doors open.

If I don't get on, I'll be late.

It doesn't matter if you're standing him up.

It matters, though.

I can go dump my fake fiancé in person. I push into the crowd getting onto the nearest subway car.

———

Two stops. Four minutes on the train, but it feels like a lifetime. I wanted to get here early, but it's almost five to eleven when the subway slows and pulls into St. George Station. I'd been clutching my phone in my hand like a security blanket, even though I can't call Toby from underground.

But now I stow it back in my clutch and take a deep breath.

The platform is busier than usual. There's a tour group of German backpackers standing right in front of me, and I move around them, looking for a guy holding flowers.

Why didn't I ask for a picture?

Maybe because that would make this real.

My pounding pulse says this is pretty damn real as it is.

I stop and take another deep breath.

Taking the breaths isn't the problem. It's letting them out that my body seems reluctant to do. Maybe hyperventilating will get me out of this whole thing.

Dear Nana, I meant to elope today with dear Alex, but I lost consciousness instead. Obviously am allergic to marriage. So sorry.

People keep looking at me.

I get it. I'm in a wedding dress and definitely too made up to be heading to the university. And I'm a freaking hot mess ten seconds away from a meltdown.

I turn around again, looking for—

Toby.

He's leaning back against the wall. He's wearing a black suit, white shirt, black tie. Slim-fit, all of it, making him look even taller than his usual six-foot-plus.

And there's an orchid pinned to his lapel.

A small orchid bouquet in his hand.

He pushes off the wall and walks toward me.

"Cara," he says, stopping in front of me. "You look beautiful."

I blink at him, not understanding what is happening. I mean, I get it. He's here. Alex clearly bailed.

Great, even my fake groom doesn't want me.

But how?

"I haven't seen the photographer yet," he says. His mouth keeps moving and the words slowly sink in, but the more he talks, the less in synch this whole moment is. Mouth. Words. Not matching up.

"Where's Alex?" I finally ask, cutting him off.

"I'm Alex."

"No..." All the other words slam into my brain. *We're going to have an audience in a minute. Photographer. How do you want to do this?* "You're...my Alex for today?"

"I..." He rolls his bottom lip between his teeth. "I'm Alex, period."

I look up at him, all the pieces falling together. There was never an escort. All of this adventure was carefully orchestrated for me to never have— "What?"

"We don't have a lot of time to do this, gorgeous. But I'm... an Alex. Your Alex. That wasn't the original plan, but as soon as you picked that name, I knew I couldn't let..." He shrugs and gives me a lopsided grin. "We can fight about this in a minute if you want. I've got a limo upstairs. The photographer can wait for us."

He's got a limo.

I keep repeating things in my head, hoping the echo will make sense of what's going on. "This wasn't a prank?"

"God, no." He slides his wallet out of his back pocket and flips it open. I take the California driver's license he hands me.

Tobias Alexander Hunt.

"You're actually an Alex."

"I am. And I'd like to be your Alex."

"What...How...When..." I hand back his license, then shake my head. "We can't do this."

"Of course we can."

"Toby!"

"Elope with me. For real or pretend, I don't care."

I laugh, and once the hysterical edge catches, it doesn't let go. Toby takes my arm and guides me to a corner of the platform. I lean back against the wall and he lets me laugh until my sides hurt and my eyes water. "Now *that's* crazy."

He leans in, close enough for me to get a whiff of his aftershave, which makes my heart ache, but not as much as the warm words he murmurs in my ear. "I love you."

That just makes me laugh harder, which is *awful*, because I love him, too.

But this is not the way to go about anything.

I wipe the tears from the corner of my eyes, then hiccup.

Oh, crap. When did my laughter turn to legit tears? I screw my face up and shake my head. "I'm sorry," I whisper.

Toby hands me a cotton, monogrammed handkerchief and brushes a kiss against my cheek. "No, this was a terrible idea. All on me. Shit. I take it all back."

"Don't take it back." I shake my head. "Not the last part."

"All on me?"

"No, before that." I press the cotton to my cheeks, to the corner of my eyes, then take a deep breath and wiggle my fingers between us, finding his hands as I blink up at him. "Did you mean it? About..."

"Loving you?" He gives me a lopsided grin. "Yeah."

"When...How...Why?"

"Over sushi. Probably before the kiss, but that definitely helped solidify some things. In hindsight, probably since you were barely legal and wicked smart."

"Toby!"

His grin gets broader. "Don't hate me for that. I never fantasized about you naked until after we kissed. Definitely legal, then."

"Last night wasn't just a one-time thing?"

"I sure as hell hope not."

"I don't know what to say."

"Say you'll marry me. Just the fake thing you've already set up. Let's tell your family we eloped, because we're crazy, and crazy about each other, and see where things go from there."

I search his face for any sign of doubt or sympathy or charity. I find none. "Yes."

"Yes?" He drops his forehead to mine and grins. "Yes."

"I'll fake marry you, Tobias Alexander Hunt."

"That's a start." He cups my cheek and kisses me, softly at first, then deeper when I part for him. Butterflies take flight in my chest as his lips move against mine, soft and sweet and oh so knowing.

Click. Flash.

"You must be the happy couple," calls the photographer from the other end of the platform. "I was wondering where you'd gone."

Toby pulls me close. "Show time."

CHAPTER NINETEEN

TOBY

I CAN'T STOP TOUCHING Cara, because *I can touch her*. And every time I do—when I take her hand, brush my fingers up her arm, or hold her close—she gives me the biggest smile.

Apparently, this isn't the first elopement photo shoot the photographer, Tanya, has done. After she introduces herself, she runs us through the basic shots she likes to get. To get us a good set of thirty pictures, she wants to take a couple hundred, so she encourages us to just do our thing and let her click-click-click without too much interference.

Easier said than done, like this entire thing.

"When did you get here?" Cara asks as she snuggles into my side in the limo, Tanya at the other end of the stretch vehicle.

"Yesterday morning," I murmur against her temple.

I don't miss the way she quietly sucks in a breath. "So last night?"

"I was just down the road."

She ducks her head, her cheeks pink.

"I'll make up for that this afternoon," I promise, and a shudder racks through her body. "If you want."

Instead of answering, she presses even closer and tips her face up so we can kiss.

The ride to the location on campus where we are meeting the officiant only takes a few minutes. It would have been a ten-minute walk at most, but I'm glad we have the car. As soon as we're done with the photographer and the officiant, I'm going to want to be alone with Cara—and the back of a limo is plenty enough privacy for my purposes.

The photographer gets out first, giving us a moment alone which I take full advantage of. Then I step out and offer my hand for my pink-cheeked, bright-eyed bride.

"You've thought about how we're going to explain this to Ben?" Cara asks. The lilt of her voice and the lightness to her step promises she doesn't really care if I have.

That's my troublemaker.

"I have. I'm going to tell him I fell in love with you in the most unexpected, ordinary way. That one phone conversation turned into another and another, each one longer than the last, because talking to you became the most important part of my day." I cup my hand around her upper arm and point toward the official-looking guy heading our way. "I'm going to tell your brother the truth. That I woke up one day and realized I loved you, and knowing you'd want an elopement on your terms, I came to Toronto and surprised you."

"You're going to tell him the truth," she whispers. "So we don't need to lie."

"And because it's a pretty decent love story, too. Is that our guy?"

She nods. "I think so. Mr. Graham?"

"Ms. Russo, a pleasure. And this is your unconventional beau?"

She laughs. "I must apologize, Mr. Graham. It turns out I'm the unconventional one. Toby—I mean, Alex—is a closet romantic."

I extend my hand. "Tobias Alexander Hunt. The romantic, at your service."

We get unofficially married under a stone archway.

"Do you, Tobias Alexander Hunt, commit your life to this woman? Do you take her to be your partner in all meanings of the word, to support her and nurture her in her life's endeavors?"

"I do."

"And do you, Cara Elizabeth Russo, commit your life to this man? Do you take him to be your partner in all meanings of the word, to support him and nurture him in his life's endeavors?"

She nods before saying, "I do."

As the officiant flips a page in his leather folder, we exchange a look that replaces any other vows we might need to make. *What about Australia?* I ask her. *We'll figure it out*, she promises back.

And we will.

"As we do not have an exchange of rings—"

"We do, actually." I flash Mr. Graham an apologetic smile for interrupting. "I wanted to surprise Cara."

"Cara's surprised," my bride says faintly, her eyes wide.

I reach into my inside pocket and snag the platinum band, yellow diamonds set flush inside the woven design. I don't need the officiant's script for this part. "Cara, I give you this ring as a symbol of my endless love, our enduring friendship, and the adventures still to come."

She holds out her hand, and I slide it onto her shaking ring finger. Then I keep going, drawing her into my arms so I can dip her back and seal my promise with a kiss.

The officiant waits until we break apart, then he gives us an approving nod. "I now pronounce you officially committed in a way that makes you happy and still pleases your family."

Cara blushes. "About that..."

He waves her off. "Don't worry about it. I've had stranger requests. And who knows. Maybe one day you'll want to make it official, and if you do, then you know how to contact me."

I shake his hand, then Cara slips an envelope out of her clutch and hands it over.

"Thank you again," she murmurs.

He departs, and we're left with the photographer, who takes one look at my face and suggests just a few more poses there under the archway.

"That sounds great," I manage to growl, and Cara's blush deepens.

I'm already counting the seconds until I get to explore just how far it extends beneath that dress.

CHAPTER TWENTY

CARA

TOBY DOESN'T SAY anything on the short drive to the Park Hyatt, just holds me close. Every muscle in his body is engaged, flexed, and ready for action.

Blush-inducing action that I can't wait for.

I consider telling him we could go to my place, but then I remember my blanket-tossing fit that happened while looking for my phone. My bedroom looks like a bomb went off.

We can wait until tomorrow for Toby to discover his fake wife is a lousy housekeeper.

He holds my hand as we cross the lobby. When we get in the elevator, he presses me against the paneled wall and kisses me senseless. And then when we're finally high above the city, he carries me, both of us laughing, over the threshold of the Algonquin Suite.

"Wow, this place is pretty," I say breathlessly as he sets me down in the bedroom.

Bedroom. Ha. I think the private part of the suite is bigger than my entire apartment. I walk through a sitting area, decorated with incredible art. Off to the side I spy a massive bathroom, and then I stop. In front of me is an imposing four-poster king-sized bed.

"Pretty doesn't really do it justice," I add weakly. I should think of a better adjective to describe the suit, but all I can see is the bed, and all I can feel is my heart hammering in my chest.

"That's how I feel about you," Toby says, stopping behind me. His hands land on my hips, then squeeze up my waist. He drops a kiss on my shoulder. "Can I unzip you now?"

I twist, and wrap my arms around his neck. "Eager, Mr. Hunt?"

"Very, Mrs. Hunt." The heat in his eyes underscores how serious he means that name.

"That's not official," I whisper.

"It is in all the ways that matter to me," he murmurs back, lowering his mouth to cover mine.

"Should we talk?" I gasp the question as he kisses down my neck. "You know, before we do something foolish like fall in love in a doomed, Romeo and Juliet kind of way?"

"I'm not taking poison with you, Cara. And I've already fallen pretty hard."

"Right."

He licks a delicate line along my collarbone, then drifts lower again, kissing across the top of my breasts, making me moan for more. "Unzipping would allow me to keep going in this fashion."

"But—"

He growls and picks me up, swinging me into his lap as he sits on the edge of the bed. He cups my cheek in his hand and gives me a stern look. "I love you. I haven't missed that you haven't said it back, so either you're scared or not there yet. I'm fine with either. I'm there. Here. All the way in, however you need me. You want to go to Australia to do a PhD? I'll visit as often as I can and we'll become masters at cyber-sex. You want to come back to Stanford? I'd support that a thousand percent. You want to live in New York? We can make that work, too. I love you, Cara. I'll give you the moon. But right now, I want to be inside you. I want to show you how good *this* can be, too. I want to make love to you."

"I haven't said it because every time you say the l-word, my brain goes a bit fuzzy and my heart threatens to explode," I whisper, pushing right up against him. "I didn't even know this was possible until like two hours ago."

"Right." His eyes go glossy as I lean in, and he gives me a sloppy grin. "Like a good fuzzy?"

"The best kind. The full-of-joy kind." I kiss the corner of his mouth. "I love you too. I. Love. You. And I have no doubt *this* will be good."

He takes another kiss, this one plundering and deep, and when his hands slide back up my spine, I don't stop him from unzipping me.

He spreads his legs wider beneath me as my dress puddles around my waist. His hands slide around my torso to cup my small breasts, leaving a restless trail of need on my skin. I lean into his touch, aching for more already.

"Let me see you," he says, his voice coarse.

I shiver as I lean back, but the loss of his touch is more than made up for by the heat in his eyes.

Slowly, he eases us back together, his mouth falling on my collarbone this time. He lifts me by the waist, pivoting us both until I'm lying on my back. He carefully slides my dress down my legs, then he's on top of me, his tongue tracing first one nipple, then the other.

My skin sizzles where he licks, and aches everywhere else. And not even for a second do I worry about the fact he's stripped me down to my panties and he's still fully dressed.

I had no idea it could be this good, or this easy.

I kick off my heels so I can wind my legs around him and hold him against me. He pulls hard, sucking more of my flesh into his mouth, and when I arch into it because *oh yes that feels amazing*, he groans.

A deep, guttural, hungry sound that does strange and wonderful things to my heart.

He pulls off with a wet pop and lifts his head. "When you said you're inexperienced..."

I reach down and touch his mouth, distracted by how shiny it is and how good it felt on my breasts. "Mm-hmm?"

"How gentle do I need to be?"

I try to smile, but it's hard because of the blast of desire that zooms through me at the question. Slowly, I shake my head. "No need to be gentle. I've done this a couple of times, it's just never been this good. So...not *this*. But sex, I've—"

He presses his face against my belly, cutting me off. I stroke my fingers through his hair, the strands silky and just long enough to hold on to.

Toby is kissing his way down my almost naked body.

Toby. Me. Naked.

In all the ways that matter, this is my first time. I don't want him holding back.

"Toby..." I roll beneath him. "Show me everything."

His fingers press into my hips, hard. He tugs my panties down, then his mouth covers my sex. I cry out at the first wet, hot swipe of his tongue. It's incredible, and I'm shameless as I writhe against him.

"Ah, Cara," he growls before licking deeper, right to my entrance. I'm slippery there, and he deftly pulls that slickness to my clit.

Your clit's getting hard, isn't it? Hard and needy. I want that on my tongue. I want to feel you throb for me.

I thought that had been dirty talk, not a promise he'd make good on at the first possible second. And yet here we are, my clit throbbing and hard, just for him.

"Touch yourself," he says as he presses his face into my inner thigh. He drags in a growly breath, then pushes off the bed. He looms above me, big and broad, and he ruthlessly strips off his clothes. "Cara. Touch. Your. Self."

I rub my hand against my lower belly, then my inner thighs. I spread my legs for him, and only when he growls at me again, do I slide my fingertips over my folds.

I gasp at how wet I am, dripping and ready.

Toby pulls a condom from a drawer before joining me again on the bed. "Make that sound again," he whispers, kissing me on the neck, right behind my ear. "That little surprised sound."

"It's all a wonderful surprise," I murmur back. "And shouldn't you be naked?"

His erection strains against my hip through the stretchy cotton of his boxer briefs. "I don't want to rush."

"Toby." I laugh weakly. "Please rush. Please make me come in a screaming fit ten seconds from now. I have complete faith we'll be able to do it again and again, all afternoon long."

"And evening."

"The weekend, too." I reach for his waistband and push it low on his hips, running my fingers over the darker hair at the bottom of his very happy trail. "Can I?"

He rolls onto his back and throws one arm over his eyes, then drags it away. "Yes. Please. No. Wait—"

"Too late." I crawl on top of him and kiss his handsome face. "Two can play at this game, Mr. Hunt."

"Take off my shorts now—"

I kiss him again to shut him up, then cover his mouth with my fingers as I try to kiss my way down his body.

I don't get very far before he's flipped me again.

My breath catches in my throat as the heat ramps up between us. Together we get him all the way naked, then he rolls a condom over his impressively thick erection. I'm staring and I can't help it. He's huge and it's been three years since the last time I did this—and that fumbling attempt had been with a much smaller penis.

Tell him to be gentle, my inner scaredy-cat urges.

But the rest of me, over-heated and achy, is more than willing to take every last inch. My hips lift toward him of their own accord, and he fits us together, the heavy crown of his cock dragging over my clit and through my folds a few times before he gives in to my whimpers and notches his erection against my entrance.

His first pulse stretches me open, and his second push brings with it a welcome pressure that has me babbling a stream of begging gibberish.

Yes, yes, fill me, more, oh there, ah...

Each press of his hips is sure. Not gentle, but not rough, either. I rock up, ready for more, and he holds me down. "Steady," he growls.

"Don't hold back," I whisper, and he groans a strained laugh.

"You're so damn tight, Cara. I'm not holding back, I'm trying not to lose my mind."

"Lose it." I arch up against him as he fills me again, deeper still. "I'm so close."

I hadn't known I was empty until he was inside me, and now I want that thing that comes next, that I can see in the near distance. Shimmery and fantastic. I want that while he's inside me.

He shifts over me, his arms bulging and his shoulders flexing as he braces one hand beside my head and uses the other to lift my hips.

Oh. *There.* "Toby..."

"Yeah. So close, too. I'm going to fill you up, Cara. Make you mine."

"Please, please, please." I bite my lip and close my eyes as the pleasure swirls tighter, faster inside me. His breath brushes against my mouth and I part for him. He soothes the bite mark on my lower lip, then slides his tongue into my mouth.

Sweat slicks between our bodies as he surges into me, pinning me against the bed. He kisses and fucks me with growing abandon. Each thrust is harder than the last, each kiss sloppier. I wrap my arms around his neck and weave my fingers into his hair, clinging to him as his cock wakes up every nerve ending deep inside my body.

When my orgasm comes, it's tight and hot, an implosion first, followed by an explosion of sensation. There's a moment of deafening silence as I tumble into it, then as it goes boom, everything is in hyper relief. The look on Toby's face, the sounds he's making, the rub of our bodies together and the heavy throb of him coming deep inside me.

He holds me tight as he twitches, then kisses me quickly before pulling away to get rid of the condom.

"Who knew sex was actually as amazing as people say?" I flop backward, breathless as I laugh in wonder. He joins me again on the bed and I lace my fingers through his. "Like really, that exceeded all the hype."

"It's not normally that good," he says, his voice uncharacteristically full of gravel. "Give yourself a lot of credit for how off-the-charts hot that was."

"Okay." I grin at him. "But really...I had no idea." I run my fingers along his square jaw and up onto his beautiful mouth. I flick my gaze up to his eyes, which are locked on my face. "I'm never going to let you put clothes on."

"You're ready do it again, aren't you?" The fondness in his

gaze is sweeter than any dessert in the world. Which reminds me...

"We should call for room service because you're going to need fuel in a major way."

"Sure." He tugs me close. "And then we should probably call your family."

"Tomorrow."

"Today."

"Fine. But later." I kiss him softly, then mouth my way down his jaw, his neck, and onto his chest. "I really liked your mouth on me. Now I want to repay the pleasure."

His eyes hood and he strokes his hand over my hair. "Yeah?"

I nod. "What wedding night—or afternoon—would be complete without an innocent, show-me-how-to-do-this-right blow job from your favorite troublemaker?"

His answering groan is everything I didn't know I was missing, and all I need.

CHAPTER TWENTY-ONE

TOBY

CARA CALLS HER NANA FIRST. She burrows under the lush cotton sheets, so only her head is peeking out, and she screws her face into a tight wince as she waits for her grandmother to answer the phone.

I gently rub the back of her neck.

"Nana," she says softly. "It's Cara. I have some news." She bites her lower lip. "I got married today. I've eloped."

She nervously rolls her ring around her finger as her grandmother reacts.

"Well, that's the whole point of an elopement. Not telling anyone." She swallows hard. "I didn't want a big wedding." She glances at me as I squeeze her shoulder gently in agreement. "We didn't want a big wedding."

"You and Alex?" That response is clear enough for me to hear through the phone, and I try not to laugh.

"No...Not Alex."

There's a pause, then the response is sharp and crystal clear. "Cara, marriage is not something to play around with."

"Are you sure? Because you were pretty happy to push me into one that I didn't want."

I lean in to catch Nana's response. "I don't understand. Who did you marry today?"

Cara gives me a half-smile. "Someone I've had a crush on for longer than I realized. Someone who is an amazing friend to me."

"Another mystery man?"

She lifts her eyebrows in question to me. I shake my head and she laughs gently. "No, Nana. Not a mystery any more. I've fallen in love with Ben's friend Toby."

Then she tells her grandmother what I said earlier. How we've had a long-distance friendship that turned into something more serious without her fully realizing it, and as she started dating Alex, she found herself thinking about me more and more.

God, I hope that's true.

"We're both coming to the beach house for the Fourth of July, I promise," she says before ending the call.

She launches herself into my arms, burying her face in my neck.

"That wasn't so bad, was it?" I murmur against her hair.

"You can call Ben." I hold out my hand, and she gives me her phone. Then she steals it back. "No, I should do it."

I circle her hand with my fingers. "Or we could do it together."

She nods. "Okay."

She finds his name in her contacts list, then puts the phone on speaker as it begins to ring.

"Hello?"

I clear my throat. "Hey, Ben."

"Toby?" I can practically hear him pull the phone away

from his ear and look at the screen. "Why are you calling me from Cara's phone?"

"Funny story," Cara says, leaning her head against mine. "Toby's in Toronto right now."

"Did you drag him out for dinner?"

She grins. "No, we haven't made it to a restaurant yet."

"Don't be too much of a pest," he says, and her mouth drops open, her eyes bright as she twists to look at me.

"Really not a concern," I deadpan. "I came up here to see her. To surprise her, actually. We, ah..." For all my bravado about it being no-big-deal to tell Ben I fell in love with his sister, it really is a big deal. I want to get this right. "You might want to sit down for this."

"I'm good." His voice is tight now. Shit.

"Ben," Cara says softly. "Toby and I got married today. We eloped."

"Because I've fallen in love with her," I add quickly.

"You fell in love with my sister." A hard, disbelieving statement.

I press on, because I sure as shit did. "We've known each other for years, Ben. And over the last month, we started talking a lot more. Then this push by your grandmother for her to get married brought my feelings to the forefront."

"Just like that."

"Ah, hell no. It was big and complicated and serious. But also unavoidable. I love her, man. So I bought her a ring and came up to Toronto to surprise her with it."

"Best surprise ever." Cara sighs as she smiles. "Oh, Ben, say you understand."

"Well, I'm happy if you're happy, I guess. Elana's going to have your heads for eloping," he says gruffly. "Did you at least take pictures?"

"I hired a photographer." Cara's eyes go wide after admitting that, but Ben doesn't ask about the timeline on that part of it.

"Have you told her yet?"

"She's my next call. I phoned Nana first, then we called you."

He grunts. "Toby?"

"Yeah, man."

"You better really love her."

"I really do."

"Good." He laughs. "Jesus Christ. I knew something was going on when we went for sushi."

I look at Cara, and we both start laughing. "We didn't," she admits. "It really took us both by surprise."

"I feel kind of bad for that Alex guy you were seeing," he grumbles, and that just makes us laugh harder.

I slide my fingers into Cara's silky soft hair and gaze at her pretty, open face. "He'll survive."

She nods. "That was a temporary thing anyway. I think I just needed to, uh, go through that to understand that Toby was who I really wanted."

"That's dangerously sappy, so I'll let you go before this gets weird," her brother says. "Call Elana ASAP."

"I will."

"Hey, Ben," I say. "Maybe don't tell Jake or Marcus just yet. Or anyone else. Just family until we've gotten together on the Fourth of July, okay?"

"Sure."

When Cara ends the call, she gives me a curious look. "Why don't you want to tell your other friends? I'm not complaining, of course. This is all overwhelming."

"For exactly that reason. When Jake started dating Jana, we

were all over him. He'd love to pay back that scrutiny. We could use a week of it just being the two of us."

"Ha. That's what I would have said about telling my family."

"That's different," I murmur as I kiss her lips. "They're my in-laws now. I need to keep them on my good side."

She kisses me back, then lifts the phone again. "One more in-law to call, then."

This is all her. I stretch out and offer her my arm to lean into as she waits for her sister to pick up.

"Elana, it's Cara. I have some news, and I think you do, too. Want to trade?"

There's a pause, then she giggles. "Ben and I guessed weeks ago. We should get a gold star for keeping it to ourselves. I'm so excited for you! When are you due?"

Another pause, then she groans. "Okay, fair is fair. And Nana will probably be calling you shortly anyway. I... Well, I got married today." She wrinkles her nose. "Yes, to a real person. Oh my *God*, I can't believe you would think that I would make up a groom. That's *terrible*."

I bite my knuckle to keep from laughing, and she pokes me in the side. I point to the living room part of the suite, and she waves me off.

"It's *Toby*, okay? ... Toby Hunt. Yes, Ben's best friend. No, I'm not making this up. ... Yes, he's very cute."

I turn and give her a raised-eyebrow look at that, and she blushes.

"Very, very cute. He showed up and surprised me with a ring. So we eloped...No, I don't want to do a whole other wedding. Yes, I know you would...okay, maybe something in the Hamptons over the Fourth of July weekend. No, not fancy..."

I leave her to hash out the not-a-wedding, but-still-fancy celebration Elana wants to throw in Sagaponack when we're all there. I head downstairs to get a secret wedding dinner for my bride. The wife of my heart.

I have in-laws now. And they're only slightly bat-shit crazy. Plus, I'm already like a brother to her brother...we just can't talk about women the same way ever again.

Bring on the holidays.

CHAPTER TWENTY-TWO

CARA

IT'S hot in the Hamptons, and not only because my fake husband has his right hand curled around my upper thigh as he deftly drives out of the East Hampton airport.

It will take at least half an hour to get to the beach house today, with traffic crawling in all directions.

That should be just enough time to convince Toby not to fly back to Toronto with me after this weekend.

We've been fake-married for two weeks, and we've each done the cross-country flight once. We need to pace ourselves and find a sustainable long-distance routine that will work for at least the next year, and probably longer.

I still dream of living in Australia.

Now I wake from those dreams feeling like a traitor to love, though.

"What are you thinking about?" he asks as he rubs his fingertips along the hem of my shorts.

"You should go back to Palo Alto after the weekend."

"I will," he says gently. "By way of Toronto."

"I'll come and visit at the end of the month."

"Mm-hmm."

"So we don't really need to—"

"Need to? No, of course we don't *need* to. But if we'd had a big wedding, I'd have taken two weeks off so we could have a honeymoon in Fiji. A few stolen days here and there over the summer is a perfectly reasonable variation on the honeymoon time."

I swallow hard. "We could still do the Fiji thing at some point."

"Like in a year, when you move to Australia?" He gives me a sideways glance, all warmth and understanding.

"I don't know. Maybe."

"We'll make it work. Maybe I'll spend a few years focusing on an Asian expansion out of my Sydney office."

"You don't have a Sydney office."

"Obviously an oversight I should correct immediately." He lifts his hand to shift gears again as traffic starts moving, then returns it immediately to my thigh. He squeezes gently. "Are you really worried about me missing too much work?"

I laugh. "Right. I guess nobody's going to fire you."

"I'll give myself a stern talking to at my next self-performance review."

"No, I'm not worried, exactly. I just don't want this to become too much." My chest tightens as I say that. He is just my fake husband, after all.

"Not a concern from my end, I promise."

I cover his hand with mine, and the ring he bought me glitters in the sunshine streaming through the window. That's not fake.

He takes the Bridgehampton exit and heads toward Sagaponack.

My pulse picks up.

"It's going to be fine," he says, not taking his eyes off the road ahead.

"Of course it is," I whisper. Will they see? Will they know?

The next time Toby reaches for me, it's not my leg he curves his fingers around. It's the back of my neck, his fingers gently rubbing up into my hairline as he pets me like a nervous kitten.

He sees me. He knows.

We drive through the village in silence, and by the time we see the dunes around my family's beach house, I don't think I could say anything else. I concentrate on the hypnotic stroking of his fingers on my skin and try to convince myself nothing else matters.

"We could keep going," he says completely straight-faced.

I choke on unexpected laughter. "And find a place to stay on the long weekend?"

"I have some resources at my disposal."

The understatement of a century. "What, would you buy a house in Sag Harbor so we could hide on the other side of the island?"

"Excellent plan." He accelerates, making as if to overshoot the beach house, and I giggle.

Then I lean over and squeeze *his* thigh. "No. Let's go and face the music."

He pulls into the drive, an easy, cocky grin on his face, and I shake my head.

My sister's car is already here. My brother hasn't arrived yet, which floods my body with relief. "Music-facing may have a slight delay. It doesn't look like Ben and Nana have arrived yet."

"The traffic was crazy. I'm glad we decided to fly into East Hampton and rent a car instead of coming out from the city with them." Toby squeezes my hand. "While we're waiting for them, why don't you sneak me into your bedroom?"

"That's an excellent idea." I grin and we both leap out of the car at the same time. Toby pops the small trunk and we grab our weekend bags, then we climb the stairs to the front door.

Elana is waiting for us on the other side. I'm not sure how she thought she was going to hide the fact that she's pregnant again, her tiny baby bump has totally popped.

"My baby sister, the bride!" she exclaims, throwing her arms wide before squeezing me tight. "I promise I haven't gone overboard—"

"That's code for you totally have, right?"

She makes a shushing sound and hugs me even tighter. "But we're going to have the most amazing dinner tomorrow night. Totally casual. Clambake and dancing on the beach."

"We can celebrate all the things," I murmur. "My new husband, your new baby..."

"Jake just got engaged," Toby says, looking up from his phone. He turns the screen toward us. "Like a minute ago."

I pump my fist in the air. "Yes! More to celebrate!"

Elana frowns. "Maybe we can have a breakfast for them the day after... try to keep this—"

"Nope," I say, blissfully spinning my big sister in a circle. "All the things. Happy night tomorrow. This is perfect."

She shakes her head at me, but lets it go as she reaches for Toby. His turn to be squeezed to death. "You married my baby sister? In secret?"

He grins at me over her shoulder. "I did."

I miss what she says, but from the exaggerated face he pulls, I'm thinking it's some kind of threat. "Elana, let him go."

He whispers something in her ear before she releases him, and they're both smiling when she turns around.

I roll my eyes and tug him toward the stairs. "Holler when Ben pulls into the driveway with Nana, okay?"

She laughs. "I will. And remember that my children are just outside, so don't be too loud."

I groan. "Well now we're not going to be loud at all. Thanks for that."

We stop on the landing and look out toward the beach. Sure enough, there's Elana's husband racing back and forth with her boys.

Toby sets his hands on my hips. "I can be very quiet," he murmurs in my ear.

I twist my head around. "What did you say to Elana?"

"Same thing that I tell you every day. You are the best, most unexpected gift I've ever been blessed with, and I'll never hurt you."

My heart melts. Okay, quiet it is.

I have the smallest room at the back of the second floor, but it has a small balcony and a private bathroom, so I've never minded the cramped quarters before.

Now, as we set our bags on the single chair in the corner, and bump into each other navigating around the bed, I start to second guess my choice. There are ten bedrooms in the house, and they won't all be full. We could move...

"Do you want a shower after all that travel?" Toby runs his fingers through my hair, then brings them back to my neck and rubs. "We can conserve water."

"Later," I say, turning in his arms. "I don't want to be in there when Nana arrives."

"I've met your grandmother. She's not that scary."

"You haven't met her when the empire is on the line. You are going to be grilled."

"I'll pull my public filings up on my tablet so she can see my estimated net worth."

"It's not funny."

"It's hilarious. Take a deep breath. There's no need to go spinning. What would you have done if you'd actually hired an escort and brought him here this weekend?"

I bury my face in his chest. "Can you imagine what a disaster that would have been? And you'd be just down the hall. We'd have had phone sex, and then I'd have an actor here with me."

I'm mortified just thinking of the fake love triangle I almost found myself caught up in.

Toby is shaking with quiet laughter. "I'd have glowered the entire time. We'd have ended up on the beach late at night, and I wouldn't be able to resist kissing you."

"You'd be the other man?" Now I'm laughing, too, because it didn't happen, so it's fine, but it almost did.

"I'd keep him up late drinking, and wake him up early go golfing, so he never got a minute alone with you in this room."

"I'd have picked another room," I whisper. "With a bigger bed. And a couch. And floor space."

"You'd have made him sleep on the floor?" He gives me a look of mock horror.

"I'd have taken the couch, of course. We'd only have stayed one day. I'd have made up a reason to go back to Toronto as soon as possible."

"It sounds terrible."

"Awful."

He cups my face in his hands and gives me a slow, serious smile. "It wouldn't have happened. Because you are mine, Cara. And I am yours."

"That was a big risk you took..."

"Hindsight being what it is, maybe we could have both gone about it differently, but I'm happy with where we've ended up."

I press up onto my tiptoes. "Me, too."

Ben arrives with Nana in tow two hours later. We're on the

beach when they arrive, and Elana calls for us from the deck. Toby scoops up my youngest nephew and fireman-carries him along with us.

"What?" he asks innocently as I give him a knowing look. "I'm not above using a child as a shield."

He's smart, too, because all the kids descend on Uncle Ben, which leaves Toby free to charm Nana for at least a minute before he needs to go toe-to-toe with my older brother.

"So," Nana says, eyeing him up hawkishly. "You are the young man my granddaughter has married."

"Yes ma'am."

"And you are gainfully employed?"

He grins. "You own seven percent of my company, Mrs. Russo."

"Indeed I do. You give adequate returns, but I have some thoughts on your customer service practices."

"I'd love to discuss those over a cup of tea."

She winks at him. "She prepped you."

"She did."

"She must like you, then."

I clear my throat. "I'm standing right here."

Nana frowns at me. "There's no need to be lippy, Cara."

"I can't help it," I say cheerfully. "And Toby doesn't mind."

He grins at me. "I don't mind at all."

"Well, then," Nana says, holding out her hand for me to take. "In that case, I want to hear all about this whirlwind wedding. Elana says that you wore blue?"

CHAPTER TWENTY-THREE

TOBY

I GO to follow Cara and her grandmother into the kitchen, but before I get far, Ben throws his arm over my shoulders and redirects me to the side porch.

"Let's have a beer," he says, like I have any choice in the matter.

I give him a bland look and accept the bottle he offers. "I was going to have tea with your Nana."

"This won't take long."

"Elana's already threatened to take a hit out on me should I hurt Cara, which I won't."

He shrugs. "Sure, that's one way to do it. I'd rather murder you with my own two hands."

"She'd knee-cap you for saying that, you know." I give my best friend a patient grin.

He takes a long pull of his beer and glowers at me. "Of course I do. And I'm also happy for her, if you make her happy."

"I think I do. She makes me ridiculously happy, by the way."

"Of course she does." He shakes his head. "I never should have left you alone with her in that restaurant."

I laugh. "I swear to God, that night was the first night I looked at her like that. But honestly, I think I've always loved her a little. She's so damn smart, and fearless, and adventurous."

He gives me a reluctant half-smile. "She is all of those things. Don't, uh…" He scrubs a hand over his jaw. "Don't try to hang on to her too tight, you know?"

"I know. Wherever she wants to fly, I'll follow. I've always had a bit of the wanderlust in me, too."

"I guess you have." He laughs. "Couldn't convince you to set up shop in New York, could we?"

"Tech is in California."

"Geography doesn't matter anymore, though."

I look at him carefully. "Cara's not moving back to New York, either."

He nods, his dark eyes both sad and proud at the same time. "I know." He hesitates. "You'll really follow her wherever she wants to go?"

"To the ends of the earth."

He holds out his beer and I clink my bottle against it. "Then welcome to the family, my brother."

Jake and his brand-new fiancée, Jana, arrive just before dinner.

Elana sweeps all the women into the living room, flicking a wrist at her brother. "Ben, you're in charge of getting dinner on the table. Please?"

Ben laughs. "I love how you add that question at the end, like there's even a chance you'd let me say no."

"We have weddings to discuss," she says regally.

"Fair enough." He leads us into the kitchen, where Elana has a binder detailing every meal.

I run my finger over the careful notes for tonight. "Your sister is a force of nature."

"I know. She's thinking about running for office, too."

"Jesus." I laugh.

Jake leans back against the counter and crosses his arms. "I'll donate."

"Well, yeah, of course, count me in. And Marcus will help with her environmental platform, of course. But doesn't she have enough on her plate?"

Ben just lifts his hands in the air. "What my sisters want, my sisters get. That's all I worry about."

Jake laughs and thumps me on the shoulder. "And his little sister wants you, huh?"

"We already did this. You missed the threats on my life. We're all good now." I've got a sloppy, stupid-happy grin on my face, and I don't care.

"You could have told me it was Cara who you eloped with when we were texting earlier."

"We'd just arrived. I was busy defending my honor to her older siblings."

Jake glances around toward the living room. "What do you want to bet they have my wedding all planned out by the time Ben gets the steaks grilled?"

"No doubt. Have you guys picked a date?"

"We're thinking Thanksgiving. It's our one-year anniversary, give or take, and winter dates may be easier to come by in the city. Although we could follow your lead and just elope."

I keep silent, because it's none of their business that Cara and I haven't *just* done anything.

We've begun something, though. And when the time is right, we'll finish it in our own way.

The next morning, we both wake up while the house is still quiet. Gray light filters through the window. "If we hustle down to the beach, we could probably catch the sunrise," Cara whispers, her eyes sparkling. "We've never shared one of those."

"Have we shared a sunset?" I ask as I pull on jeans and toss her a hoodie.

"Three of them. Well, two that we could see, and then, uh..." She blushes. "It was dusk when we went for that walk in Brooklyn."

I drop my gaze to her mouth. Our first kiss. And then we both gamely tried to walk away, even though it changed everything. "I remember." I glance back at her eyes. "But the other two?"

"Dinners out west. When I was in school." Her cheeks stay pink. "You have excellent taste in restaurants with amazing views."

"And even better company." I reach for her and she takes my hand. Quietly, we sneak downstairs and out the back door.

The sun has broken the horizon to the east, and we walk down the beach in that direction, watching it slowly climb into the sky, bringing with it a bloom of color.

"I didn't have a crush on you back then," Cara says quietly. "It wasn't like that. It was just nice. That's why I remember those dinners."

"And the views helped."

She laughs. "Sure. Yes. But you've always seen me."

I squeeze her hand in mine and rub my thumb against her skin. "It was easy to see you. I've always liked you. Before I loved you. Before it would have been appropriate to love you. I don't remember the restaurants we went to or the views, but I remember everything we talked about. Your ideas, your assignments, your frustrations."

She slides her fingers out of mine and twirls away, jogging down to the water. I chase her, and she dodges and weaves up and down the beach until I catch her. My arms slide around her waist as she throws her hands in the air, and I spin us both.

"You've always been the most beautiful girl in the world to me," I admit. "Even when I was firmly in protective older friend mode. And if you'd come on to me, I don't know that I would have been able to say no."

"Then it's for the best I only saw you as a mentor back then, right?"

Heat crawls through my chest. "Yes."

"But not now," she says on a breath, her lips twisting in a shy, happy smile. "You said I should wait for someone who lights me up inside. You do."

My attention keeps snagging on her soft, pink mouth. It did back then, too. Secrets I kept from myself, apparently. "I also said you should wait for a kid to get down on one knee, and I forgot to do that part."

"I forced your hand a bit."

"It's never too late." I kiss her as I set her back down, then I lower myself to one knee. I take her hand, with my ring already on it, and I gaze up at her. "Cara, will you marry me? For real?"

"Yes," she breathes. "Although everyone already thinks we did."

We did in all the ways that matter. "Let's keep the same date. Marry me next year."

"Just make it official?"

"Secretly so." I sit back on the sand and tug her down. She straddles my lap, and I kiss her knuckles before turning her hand over and kissing her open palm. "We can do it sooner if you want."

She shakes her head. "I love the idea of doing it next year."

"Might be the perfect time, right before you move on to your next adventure."

Her eyes soften. "I might not go far."

"No." I catch her chin gently between my fingers. "Cara, go as far as you want. Fly like the wind. Please. I'll follow." I exhale roughly. "I told Ben you—we—wouldn't move back to New York City. He already knows you need adventure. He challenged me to not hold you back from that. And I never would. But I need it, too. I've spent the last thirteen years in California. And it's been amazing. But I'm ready to do something new, too."

She leans in and brushes her lips against mine. Her eyelids flutter shut as she takes my mouth, and I let her consume me.

This is going to be our life for the next year. Stolen moments. A honeymoon in fragments.

By the time she finishes her degree in Toronto, I'll find a way to take the next step together, so we have more time.

My thoughts scatter as she works her way under the hem of my shirt and slides her fingers over my flexing abs. Awareness prickles on my skin, sparking deeper, more primal wants.

She breathes against my mouth as she glances between us, and her hand moves lower. Heat surges through me as she tentatively strokes my dick through my jeans. My cock immediately thickens for her, and she gives a soft, pleased murmur.

Of course I'm following her back to her place for a few days after this family vacation. We need more time to explore and discover each other.

I'm not that experienced. We're making up for a lot of lost time.

I catch her wrist before she gets my fly undone. "Whoa. Maybe let's head back to the house."

"Right." She kisses me again, smiling as she teases her tongue against mine. "In a minute."

"In a minute, I'll be coming all over your hand." I fist my other hand in her hair and tug gently. "And I'd rather be deep inside you when I do that, wouldn't you?"

Her pupils dilate as she nods. "Uh-huh."

"Then take one last look at the sunrise."

She's still giggling when I press her into the thankfully private shower in her tiny bedroom.

"Turn on the water," I tell her as I shove my jeans down my legs.

She points back to the bedroom. "Condoms."

"Plural?"

"Just in case." She catches her lower lip between her teeth, and I sprint to my bag. I'll bring the whole damn box. *Just in case.*

The shower stall is full of steam when I get back. As I step inside, Cara plasters herself to me, and we go from zero to sixty just like that.

I push her against the slick tiles and spread my legs wide, holding her perched just above my eager erection. He can wait a damn minute. I cup her breast and roll my thumb over her nipple.

"You wanted to do this on the beach?" I ask her, licking away a line of water droplets from her neck.

"Not this. Just a little touching."

I squeeze, kneading her soft flesh. "I'm touching."

"Toby..." She groans and rolls her hips. "Please."

I grin. "Not that fast. We'll have to be social all day. I want to get my fill of you and your sweet touches now." I rock against her. We'll fuck soon enough. Slow and hard and fast, too, at the end. But first, she was teasing me. I want more of that. I set her down, then step back, leaning against the other wall.

I spread my arms wide. "Touch away."

Her face lights up and she reaches for me. My abs first, just like on the beach. Then lower, tracing her fingertips through the grooves in front of my hips. My muscles bunch and tighten under her attention, and she drifts to her knees.

Oh, yes.

So far, the only blow jobs she's given me have been in bed, with her on top and in control.

But I love her kneeling in front of me. It satisfies something heady and primal deep inside me—even though of course, she's still in charge here, too.

She blinks up at me, her eyes bright and wide as she wraps her fingers around my cock. "Just touch?"

I swallow hard. "Your choice."

She slides her tongue around the head, and I thunk my skull back against the tile. All awareness in my body has converged on my rock-hard erection and the delicate licks she's laying on it. Soft, velvet teases.

My balls tighten up, and my throbbing tip slicks with pre-come. Before I can tell her to lick that up, she wraps her mouth around the entire head and pulls gently as she begins to stroke me.

Up, suck. Down, lick. In between each stroke, a wide-eyed, pleased glance up at me.

Fuck yeah, I'm pleased too. "You're so good at that," I murmur, pushing a wet strand of hair off her cheek. "Take me a little deeper. That's my girl. God, Cara, yes. Your mouth. Ah..."

I pump my hips gently as she swallows more of my length, bringing her lips all the way to her fingers. In and out. Tight and hot and perfect.

When she pulls off with a slurp, I lurch from the loss. But

she returns immediately with a condom, and I watch through lust-hazed eyes as she rolls it down my length.

Then I lift her up again and press her back against the wall, my legs pushing her thighs open. I stroke through her folds, testing that she's ready for me. I find her wet, slick, hot.

We're both breathing hard as I push up, spearing into her and stretching her pussy wide.

Her breathy moan as I bottom out inside her makes me crazy.

"So good," she whispers, and that's even better. "How is this so good?"

Because love. Because friendship. Because kismet and chemistry and fearless promises.

Promise me you won't marry some random guy. I didn't have any right to make that demand, but I'm so damn glad I did.

"Only with you," I growl, thrusting into her again. She wraps her wet limbs around my body as I surge us together. Her breasts mash against my chest, her mouth latches onto my neck, and I lose myself to the swirl of the best sex of my life.

When she comes, it's a long, sustained, rippling orgasm that demands my own climax. Her body milks me with almost endless spasms, until I sag against her and my softened erection slips out of her.

My heart pounds as I hold her against me.

She looks up at me and everything stops. It's just the two of us in this moment. I can feel myself smiling at her, tender and soft. See the light in her eyes as she returns the expression.

"A sunrise and shower sex," she says softly. "Not bad for our one-week anniversary."

I catch her mouth with mine and kiss her swollen lips before reaching past her to turn off the water. "And the day is still young."

EPILOGUE

CARA

Toronto

June, again

JET LAG IS A BITCH. I'm wide awake and it's four in the morning.

"Come back to bed," Toby mumbles, circling my wrist with his fingers.

"I think I've slept as much as I can," I murmur, letting him tug me close anyway. I don't know how he does this regularly.

"Then I should do something to exhaust you again." He rolls on top of me, his body big and hard and very awake even as sleep still drips from his voice. "I didn't get a chance last night."

He did his best to keep me up, but after a marathon thirty-hour set of flights from Sydney through Dubai, and finally back to Toronto, I zonked out hard after he picked me up from the airport.

One more month, and we'll be making the journey back to Australia together.

In the end, it was Toby who made the first move down under, and I'll be the one who technically follows along. It started with our conversations in Sagaponack, and it never stopped. By Christmas, he'd announced that Starfish Instrumentation would be starting two new divisions, with headquarters in Australia and India. A commitment to the other side of the world, he said, that his company had a global vision and international commitment.

Now it's official—I'm going to continue my studies in Sydney, and we just closed on a house overlooking the beach.

A slight upgrade from my tiny, one-bedroom condo here.

The new house is a wedding present, he told me.

Tomorrow is our one-year anniversary. We're going to Toronto City Hall, and Mr. Graham, the officiant who unofficially married us the first time, is going to do it all over again. This time, with a marriage license and everything.

Our wedding date won't change. Only the year.

And then it will be a whirlwind month. Packing and moving and graduating for me, handing over North American operations to a new command team for Toby.

He'll have someone do all his packing for him. Perk of being a billionaire.

We'll have one last monthly tea with Nana in New York. I think she'll miss Toby more than me. He humors her business talk and isn't lippy in the least.

Then we'll fly around the world to our new home, where we will finally make love in our marriage bed, in the house he bought me as a wedding gift, in the city I've dreamed of living in as long as I've been an adult.

I can't wait.

"Ah, Cara, I've missed you..." Toby's voice is soft, and the words rub right against my soul as I arch beneath him.

Correction. I can wait. I will wait, always, for whatever comes next for us. Because waiting is no hardship. I've got Toby, and he's got me.

"I missed you, too," I whisper, curling my legs up on either side of his body.

His hands go to my thighs and push them open. We've come a long way in a year, and we know each other inside and out. I flex against his touch and he growls for me.

"You offered to exhaust me," I tease as he pins me down and nips at my shoulder. "Is it too early to wrestle?"

"Never." He handily flips me over and while I'm laughing at him, he kisses his way down my spine, his lips brushing over my tattoo. He loves that spot on my back. Maybe I should get another one.

I push back against him. My husband. The only man who's ever lit me up inside, and he does it all the time. His hand snakes between my legs from behind and he finds my clit. He slides it between two flat fingers, pinching the nub as I try to squirm.

"Surrender," he murmurs in my ear. I stretch out my arms and push my hips into the air, and he chuckles. "That was easy."

"I missed you," I admit, blushing. "Now fuck me."

"A week in Australia and already you're cursing up a storm. I like it." This time it's his cock that rubs against my clit, and I press my face into the bed as I moan. "Ready for me?"

"Fuck. Me."

He's laughing as he presses into me, stealing my breath. Am I ever ready for this? It's the best thing in the world.

I close my eyes as he pumps his hips, setting a sweet, slow tempo that tortures and pleases me in equal measure.

"I'm going to take my time, since I'm awake," he murmurs.

"Nice and slow and deep, just like this. Until you're begging for my thumb on your clit. Or in your ass, maybe."

I gasp. "No." But I clench around him. Maybe yes. Okay, definitely yes. "Okay."

"Hussy. I missed you too." On that, he flexes his hips, driving himself an extra bit deeper on the bottom of the thrust. "Touch yourself, then. My fingers are going to be busy."

Mr. Graham meets us in front of the brightly colored TORONTO sign in front of city hall.

"Has it been a year already?" he asks as he shakes Toby's hand. "It's a great honor to see you both again."

We hand over the license, and he slides it into his leather folder. "Same vows again?"

"Yes, please," I say, my voice surprisingly shaky.

Toby squeezes my hand reassuringly.

Mr. Graham starts with him. "Do you, Tobias Alexander Hunt, re-commit your life to this woman? Do you take her to be your partner in all meanings of the word, to support her and nurture her in her life's endeavors?"

"I do."

Those two words haven't lost their punch. My eyes well up as the officiant turns to me. "And do you, Cara Elizabeth Russo, re-commit your life to this man? Do you take him to be your partner in all meanings of the word, to support him and nurture him in his life's endeavors?"

"I do."

"As we have already had an exchange of rings..." Mr. Graham starts to move forward in the ceremony, but this time, I'm the one who's got the surprise.

I hold up my finger, then open my clutch. Damn it, I should

have practiced this part. "Actually, last year, only Toby had a ring that day." The band I've secreted away in there slips under my fingers before I grab it properly and pull it out. "Ah ha!"

Toby's mouth drops open, then he bites his lip and nods, his eyes full of warmth.

"I don't remember what you said." My voice is so thick with emotion maybe it doesn't matter—I won't be able to say much, anyway.

Mr. Graham clears his throat. "This is, uh, one of my duties." We turn toward him and his cheeks turn pink. "I wrote it down."

"Oh, excellent. Okay. What do I say?" I turn back to Toby and he holds out his hand. Unlike me, he's not shaking at all.

"Toby, I give you this ring..." Mr. Graham prompts, and I repeat it as I slide the plain platinum band over his knuckle.

"Toby, I give you this ring... As a symbol of my endless love... our enduring friendship... and the adventures still to come." I beam at him as I finish, then I throw my arms around his neck. "I can kiss him now, right? He did that last year."

"Absolutely, Mrs. Hunt. I now pronounce you husband and wife, by the power vested in me by the Province of Ontario. You may kiss your groom."

THE END

for Toby and Cara...

But Marcus's story is next. Visit my website to keep reading! And if you want to hear about the next release in this series, or any other sexy rom com news from me, join my VIP reader list at www.smarturl.it/AinsleyMail!

ABOUT THE AUTHOR

Mom by day and filthy romance writer by night, Ainsley is a three-time USA Today bestseller (Hate F*@k, Prime Minister), and super grateful for caffeine and yoga pants. Born and raised near Toronto, Ontario, Canada, she's traveled the world and come back home to write about book boyfriends with maple leaf tattoos.

www.ainsleybooth.com
www.friskybeavers.com

ACKNOWLEDGMENTS

This story was originally written for the *Love in Transit* anthology, which was a limited time collection of stories all written to the same blurb. It was a lot of fun, and I'm so pleased to have the paperback on my shelf as a forever memory of the project that Jana Aston spearheaded and Raine Miller, BJ Harvey, Kitty French, and Liv Morris all enthusiastically jumped into.

Sadie Haller was my first reader for this story, and as usual, her eagle eyes caught so many inconsistencies. So grateful to her for that!

Thank you to Mignon at Oh So Novel for the cover for this book, and the entire series. Also to Dana Waganer for her final proofreading pass.

I'm also thankful for all my readers who were eagerly waiting for the next Frisky Beavers and Forbidden Bodyguards books, but also said, okay, sure, a billionaire rom com series, why not? You, my readers, are my favourite people in the entire world.

ALSO AVAILABLE FROM AINSLEY BOOTH

FORBIDDEN BODYGUARDS

Hate F*@k
Booty Call
Dirty Love
First Lady, His Lady
Wicked Sin

BILLIONAIRE SECRETS

Personal Delivery
Personal Escort
Personal Disaster
Personal Interest

FRISKY BEAVERS

Retrosexual
Prime Minister
Dr. Bad Boy
Full Mountie
Mr. Hat Trick
Bull of the Woods

Cover Design by Oh So Novel

All rights reserved

2017, Ainsley Booth

Printed in Great Britain
by Amazon